# HUNTER OF THE TIDE

## THE KRAKEN #3

## TIFFANY ROBERTS

# HUNTER OF THE TIDE

The Kraken Book #3
Tiffany Roberts

Cover by Cameron Kamenicky and Naomi Lucas

Edited by Cissell Ink

❀ Created with Vellum

# CHAPTER 1

*3* *61 Years After Landing*

*R*hea swam ahead of the search party, pulling Melaina along beside her. Her fingers flexed on the youngling's wrist, and it took all her willpower to keep from squeezing tighter. Embarrassment and anger blazed at the surface, but those emotions weren't what had her hearts pounding in a hollow chest, those weren't what made her throat feel tight and her limbs tremble. Fear and helplessness dominated Rhea.

*I might have lost her.*

This wasn't the first time Melaina had disappeared, or the second or third. Rhea was fast losing numbers to count her daughter's *expeditions*. It didn't seem to matter how often or vehemently Rhea explained to the child the many dangers of the sea — Melaina wouldn't be deterred. How many times could they go through this before it ended in tragedy?

Rhea turned her head to look at her daughter.

Melaina struggled to keep up with the pace set by her mother and was being dragged more than she was swimming. She held a sealed container against her chest with her free arm, undoubtedly holding some new *treasure* the girl had found — a pretty rock, or a shell, or a broken chunk of coral. Besides Melaina's gray eyes, the youngling shared her mother's looks — the same gray skin, the same delicate facial features, even a similar build, all presented in miniature — but seemed to have nothing of Rhea's temperament.

Though he was not Melaina's sire, the girl was much more like Jax, whose restless nature had earned him the name *the Wanderer*.

For a moment, Melaina met Rhea's eyes, and then looked away with discouragement and shame in her expression.

Rhea's chest constricted with guilt. Melaina was heeding some inner calling, a voice Rhea couldn't hear, an urge beyond her understanding, but it was too dangerous to allow the youngling to follow that call.

Rhea looked to her other side, where Dracchus swam nearby. He was the largest of the kraken, the strongest, and he'd been the one to lead the search for Melaina — this time, and many times before.

Noticing her attention, he turned his head toward her.

She signed with her free hand and altered her color to emphasize her sincerity.

*Thank you.*

Dracchus's brow creased. Females did not give thanks; it was for the males to protect and provide, especially with so few females, and why would any thanks be given to a male for merely fulfilling his duty? Appreciation could be shown in other ways when warranted. Ways that had the potential — however small — to produce younglings.

2

But Rhea's relief at having her daughter safe outweighed all of that, and Dracchus's willingness to search without hesitation or complaint, despite having done so countless times, meant more than Rhea could adequately express.

Finally, Dracchus dipped his head in acknowledgment and looked forward.

Rhea let her gaze linger, sweeping it over his broad shoulders and muscular arms, past his narrow hips, and along the length of his thick tentacles. Dracchus would make an excellent mate. Once, she might have considered pursuing him.

But now...now there was another who'd caught her interest.

Rhea blew through her siphons, expelling those thoughts as the Facility came into view. The main building's exterior lights illuminated only a small portion of its manmade walls, leaving the rest of the structure nothing more than a shadow amidst the gloom. The other buildings, connected to the first by tunnels, were dark smudges to either side.

The other kraken broke their loose formation, swimming toward their dens in the other buildings. Only Dracchus remained. He went to the keypad beside the door and entered the sequence all kraken were taught as younglings. The light over the door shifted from red to green, and the door slid open.

Rhea tugged Melaina into the pressurization chamber. And Dracchus followed.

Dracchus followed them inside, closing the door behind him. The water drained.

The transition from water to air was always slightly disorienting for Rhea. Her body grew heavier, felt bulkier, and her siphons gaped uselessly until her lungs expanded with their first breath. The sensation of floating always lingered for a time afterward, which only heightened how sluggish her limbs felt outside of water.

The light above the interior door went green.

"Pressurization normalized," said the computer's disembodied voice.

"Mother—" Melaina began.

"How many times must I tell you never to leave?" Rhea growled, spinning to face her daughter. Melaina flinched back. "Did you learn nothing when you were nearly killed by the razorback? When Macy nearly died to save you?" Rhea's tentacles writhed.

Melaina ducked her head, lips turned down into a frown. Her small shoulders sagged. The human, Macy, was Jax's mate, the female who finally eased his restlessness. Her arrival had thrown the kraken's world into a state of change, and the devotion she and Jax showed to one another had forced Rhea to confront her own loneliness, her own desires for lasting companionship. Rhea had come to consider Macy a friend, and Melaina was extremely fond of the human.

Rhea's stomach twisted. Had she fallen so low as to use Melaina's adoration of Macy to guilt the youngling into compliance? It hurt to see her child look so small, so defeated, but Melaina's safety was more important than anything else. Younglings were precious among the kraken because they were so rare, and females rarer still.

*But she is my daughter.*

"There could be hunters out there, searching for kraken to capture," Rhea said, softening her voice. "What would happen if they found you? You cannot keep doing this, Melaina."

"There are many dangers in the sea," Dracchus added, "and if we do not know where you are, we cannot protect you."

4

Somehow, Melaina shrank further at the male's gentle admonishment.

Dracchus pressed the button on the wall and the interior door opened. They exited the chamber, entering a long corridor. "I will tell the others that the youngling is safe."

Once Dracchus had turned down another hallway, Rhea turned to her daughter, who stood beside her with head bowed.

Sighing, Rhea lowered herself, easing her tentacles and curling them up at her sides. She brushed the backs of her fingers over Melaina's cheek. "What did you find?"

Melaina raised her head, face lighting up. She placed her container on the floor. Before she could open the lid, something thumped inside, scooting the whole thing a hand span over the floor.

Rhea tensed. "What was that?"

"I'll show you," Melaina said, removing the lid.

Rhea leaned over to look inside.

A small, scaled creature stared back at her with large, dark eyes. Its paddle-like tail swished restlessly in the water filling the container, and the whiskers protruding from its snout twitched. The creature lay on the bottom with its rear legs folded beneath it, displaying puncture wounds on its hindquarters — likely the bite of a predator. Lifting a front leg, the creature extended its paw toward Rhea, stretching the webbing between its toes.

"A prixxir?" Rhea asked, looking back to Melaina. "It is a youngling."

"He's hurt," Melaina said. "I couldn't just leave it."

Melaina reached for the creature, but Rhea caught her wrist before her fingers entered the container.

"It might bite, Melaina."

Before the youngling could reply, voices from farther down

the hall drew Rhea's attention away. A group of females rounded a corner and approached.

"Melaina!" Thana, at the front of the group, hurried over with relief in her eyes. "Dracchus just told us you were back. I am so glad to see you safe."

Another female, Aja, lowered herself beside Melaina. The prixxir moved suddenly, splashing water onto the floor, and Aja flinched back.

"What is that?" she demanded, eyes wide.

"A prixxir," Melaina said. "He's hurt."

Thana leaned forward to look into the container. "And what are you doing with it, little one?"

"I want to help it."

Rhea lowered her brow and tilted her head. "But you do not know how to care for the creature."

Melaina looked down at the prixxir, crestfallen. "I could try."

Pounding footsteps echoed along the corridor. Rhea turned toward the sound as Randall ran into the corridor from one of the intersecting halls. He skidded to an abrupt halt beneath the stares of the gathered females.

Rhea trailed her gaze over him. His cheeks and jaw were covered with a light growth of hair, and the hair atop his head was tousled. The dark blue material of his jumpsuit clung to his muscular form, hinting at the body beneath. Heat suffused her, and she gritted her teeth against a sudden wave of desire. She'd seen him without coverings when he was first brought to the Facility, and that only made her long to see him bare again. It took considerable effort to keep her skin from changing color when all she wanted to do was signal her interest to mate with him.

His bright blue eyes met hers.

He stood with his arms spread slightly to the sides, undoubtedly to make it clear that he wasn't reaching for the holstered gun on his belt. Several kraken had voiced their discomfort with Randall carrying such weaponry, but Dracchus had insisted Randall be equipped to defend himself should the need arise.

Aja spun to face Randall and growled. "What do you want, human?"

Randall lifted his hands and displayed open palms. He didn't move any closer, leaving several body lengths between himself and the females. "I didn't mean to interrupt anything. I heard they found Melaina, and just wanted to make sure she was okay."

"As you can see, she's fine. Be gone."

"Enough," Rhea snapped, glaring at Aja.

Aja twisted to narrow her eyes at Rhea. "You are defending this human? Do you side with *them?*"

"There are no sides here," Randall said. "We're all just living, right? I'm not—"

Aja lunged toward Randall. "Were it up to some of us, you would not be—"

Rhea caught Aja's arm and yanked her back, shoving her against the wall. She pinned her in place with her forearm across the other female's chest and held the claws of her other hand at Aja's throat. In her peripheral vision, Rhea saw Melaina carefully pick up her container and move behind Thana.

"Have you forgotten so easily that this human is under Dracchus's protection?" Rhea asked, voice low.

"You are as much a betrayer as he is!" Aja snarled, struggling against Rhea's hold.

Rhea caught Aja's wrists with her tentacles, forcing the other female's hands down to her side, and leaned more of her weight against her captive. She cocked her head. "Do you challenge me, Aja?"

7

Heaving through clenched teeth, Aja only glared at Rhea.

"There's no betrayal happening here, and no need for a challenge," Randall interjected. "I'm not here to cause trouble."

"Be silent, human," Rhea commanded, though gently. She didn't remove her gaze from Aja. "Do you?"

Aja shook her head sharply.

Rhea released her and moved back.

Sagging slightly, Aja rubbed at her chest with one hand. She glanced at Randall, face tight with anger and humiliation, glared once again at Rhea, and then spun away. All the females save Thana hesitantly followed her. Randall pressed himself against the wall as they passed him; none so much as looked at him while they were near.

"Has she sided with Kronus?" Rhea asked.

Thana sighed and lifted her hands, palms up. "If she has not yet, she is likely to now. I believe Leda has been whispering in her ear."

"These jealous females will start a fight they cannot win."

Thana looked at Randall. "Even threat of Dracchus's retribution will not deter some of Kronus's supporters. Though they despise Arkon, they gladly used the wounds he suffered at the hands of the human hunters as proof that humans are our enemies."

"I'm not trying to incite more violence," he said, frowning. The hunters who shot Arkon had been under Randall's command until they'd betrayed their leader. Randall still bore scars as evidence of their treachery.

"Your mere presence does that," Thana said.

"It's not like I asked to come here."

"But here you are," Rhea said. "Thana, tell the other females he is under my protection, as well. An insult to him — to any of the humans here — is an insult to me."

Randall clenched his jaw, and a crease appeared between his eyebrows. "I can't say I don't appreciate the gesture, but you don't need to welcome trouble on my behalf, Rhea."

Rhea grinned at him. "It is no trouble."

Randall's gaze dipped to her mouth. Humans had mostly flat teeth, and she supposed hers were as odd to him as his were to her.

"I am glad Melaina is safe," Thana said. She looked from Rhea to the youngling. "I will see you both soon, I hope."

Dipping her head in a silent farewell, Thana set off down the corridor in the same direction the other females had gone.

Randall offered Thana a warm, uncertain smile as she passed. Once she was gone, he ran his hand through his hair. Rhea had been tempted many times to comb her fingers through it, too, to feel its softness against her fingertips, to feel it brush along her palm.

He walked up to her, now that no obstacles remained in his path. "Like I said, I just wanted to make sure everything was okay. I'll leave you to it before I'm the cause of another fight." He turned away.

"You are a hunter," she said quickly, bringing his attention back to her.

"I was."

"Why would you think you are one no longer?"

He shrugged. "I look around me sometimes, and my brain says everything I'm seeing — this place, your people — can't be real. Kind of hard to figure out who or what I am when I haven't quite reconciled everything else yet."

"But here we are," Rhea said, spreading her arms and tilting her head. "You were a hunter before you knew of our kind. Our existence did not affect what you were, then."

"The foundation was already cracked before I found out your people were real. That discovery just served as the catalyst to break everything apart."

"But it does not change who you are here." Rhea placed a hand on her chest with fingers spread wide, over her hearts. His eyes followed her gesture and widened slightly.

"Maybe not," he replied, glancing down at his own chest, "but it made me realize I don't know who I am as well as I thought I did. Again, I appreciate it, but you don't need to worry about me. I'll figure things out. You have your own problems to deal with."

"Can you help him?" Melaina asked, lifting her container toward Randall.

He arched a brow, glancing from Melaina to Rhea and back again. "Him?"

"A hunter knows about creatures, yes?" Rhea asked.

Melaina approached Randall. "He's hurt."

Randall squatted and looked into the container. "Where did you find this? Prixxir are all over the coastlines, but I didn't think they came out this far."

Melaina's guilty glance confirmed that the girl had gone even farther from the Facility than Rhea would've suspected. Rhea cast a disapproving glare at her daughter, who quickly averted her gaze and turned back toward Randall.

"He was hurt and alone," Melaina said. "Can you help him, Randall?"

The prixxir placed a webbed paw on the side of the container and lifted its head, whiskers twitching.

Reaching down, Randall gently touched the creature; it let out a squeaking yelp and curled up on the bottom again. "I've never taken care of anything like this, Melaina. That's... It's not really what hunters do."

"But like any hunter, you watch; you learn. You know their habits," Rhea said.

His gaze shifted up to meet hers. "I've only dealt with these things on land. And I don't know how serious its wounds are, or how to treat them."

"Aymee might," Melaina said.

Randall's frown deepened. He regarded the prixxir in silence for a long while.

Perhaps it was wrong for Rhea to pressure him into accepting the responsibility, but what did she — or any kraken, for that matter — know about caring for an animal? The only sea creatures kraken interacted with were prey. The only other options were to return the prixxir to the sea, where it might perish, or kill it and use it for food.

But after the tumultuous emotions of the last few hours, Rhea couldn't bear the look of disappointment Melaina would wear if the creature died. Was it selfish of Rhea to burden Randall with her daughter's happiness?

Rhea straightened and inhaled deeply. "Please." The word felt strange as it left her lips; female kraken didn't *ask*, and they most certainly didn't *beg*.

Melaina echoed her mother.

Running a hand over his stubbly cheeks, Randall sighed. "All right. I'll figure something out. But I can't promise anything."

Melaina's face brightened with a huge smile.

"*And* I have a condition," he continued.

Rhea frowned and furrowed her brow. "What is this condition?"

"Melaina has to help take care of it."

"Yes!" Melaina exclaimed, her tentacles writhing on the floor. "I will!"

Randall lifted his eyes to Rhea in question.

Rhea nodded once.

"Good. Now, my father told me when I was little that you shouldn't name animals, because they were bound to...well, *move on*. But my sister named them anyway. I think you should give him a name. Having something that belongs to him will help him be strong."

Melaina stared down at the prixxir. The creature stared back up, shifting its attention between Randall and the youngling. Opening its mouth, it released a high-pitched call and attempted to leap out of the container; it fell back into the water with a splash.

"Ikaros," Melaina said.

"Come." Rhea placed a hand on Melaina's shoulder. "Randall will tend to it, and we will visit soon."

"Ikaros, Mother, not *it*."

Rhea raised a brow.

Melaina offered Randall a smile. "Thank you."

Despite thanking Dracchus earlier, Rhea's instinct was to tell her daughter never to thank a male; it was a male's duty to provide. But she held it in. Things were changing. The kraken were changing. And Randall wasn't a kraken, anyway. Rhea had been learning from her human friends, Macy and Aymee, and they frequently expressed appreciation to their males. Perhaps it was a good thing to do, from time to time.

"Hopefully I'll earn that thanks." Randall's smile, despite his strange human teeth, was the most charming that Rhea had ever seen. She stared at his lips and wondered what it would feel like to have them pressed against hers.

# CHAPTER 2

*A*ll was quiet as Randall walked through the empty corridors save for his own footsteps, the gentle sloshing of water in the container, and the occasional whine from the prixxir within. The creature's calls were high-pitched, chirruping, and heart-wrenching. Though some part of Randall thought it was ridiculous to empathize with an animal — his father would've called him a damned fool — he couldn't help but think he knew how Ikaros felt.

*As though things aren't grim enough, now I'm comparing myself to a baby sea-lizard.*

He grinned. Fortunately, no one was around to see it; he worried it was the expression of a desperate man losing touch with reality. The thought shouldn't have amused him that much.

He took a meandering route through the Facility; his mind wandered often lately, and he lost himself in thought as he went to check the spots Aymee frequented when she wasn't in her room — the mess hall, the infirmary, the chamber she and Arkon had cleared to use for painting.

The thought of Aymee and Arkon gave him pause. Randall had wanted Aymee from the first moment he'd seen her — she was beautiful, yes, but she was also passionate, bold, and intelligent. If circumstances had been different for them both, he liked to think he would've had a chance. They'd enjoyed one another's company on the few occasions during which they'd been able to relax. But she'd fallen for Arkon.

That had hurt a lot more than Randall had expected it would.

He searched for that bitterness, for the ache of rejection, for the constriction in his chest, but he could not find them anymore. He'd seen Aymee and Arkon together often in the weeks he'd spent here in the Facility, and it had stung every time. That sting had lessened a little with each passing day.

Somehow, Rhea had chased the last of that feeling away. She'd been kind — if sometimes overbearing — during Randall's time here, and she made little effort to hide her interest in him. While he'd recovered in the infirmary, it'd been Rhea who was there each time he woke, Rhea who'd often tended to him. Now, she'd stood up for him to other kraken without hesitation.

*And said* I'm *under* her *protection...*

The first time he'd seen her — while he was in extreme pain and on the verge of exhaustion — he hadn't known what to think. The kraken had been so new to him, then, so alien, and the females were hairless and bare, their breasts on full display. But he'd grown more accustomed to their appearances since, and he couldn't deny Rhea's exotic beauty and effortless grace. Her features were deceptively delicate, belying her impressive physical strength, and her gray skin was so soft to the touch.

His curiosity felt dangerous; was it right for him to be attracted to her? Was it natural?

Randall had spent his life hunting dangerous creatures, and

that's what the kraken were supposed to have been — prey. More threatening than anything else he'd hunted, perhaps, but wild beasts all the same. Something that needed to be killed to protect human life. Shaking that manner of thinking had proven difficult; it had been ingrained in him since childhood.

Pushing away those thoughts, he shifted his attention to his surroundings, stopping to lean into Aymee's painting room. She wasn't there, so he continued walking.

In some ways, the Facility reminded Randall of home. Like Fort Culver, this place had been constructed with clean, impersonal aesthetics favoring practicality and functionality. Despite centuries of inhabitation by the kraken, it was clear that everything in the Facility had had its place, and that everything had been arranged in a fashion that favored organization. It'd come as little surprise when he was told this place — like Fort Culver — had been utilized by military personnel.

But Fort Culver wasn't sixty-five meters below the surface of the ocean, nor was it inhabited by human-animal hybrids.

Pausing in the doorway of the mess hall — called simply the Mess by the kraken — he glanced inside. The large room, which had undoubtedly been utilized as a dining area long ago, was empty, and the kitchen beyond was dark.

As he walked toward the infirmary, he glanced down at Ikaros. The prixxir stared up at him with those wide, dark eyes, looking so small, so helpless.

"Damnit," he muttered.

His sister, Elle, would've laughed if he told her he saw his feelings reflected in the gaze of an animal, but there wouldn't have been judgment in her laughter. *This* was what she'd so often talked about. *This* was the sort of connection she'd made with so many of Halora's creatures.

He'd never thought less of her for it, though their father had little patience for what he called her *bleeding heart*. She could outpace most other rangers, was the best shot in the fort and everywhere else they'd gone, and maintained her cool better than anyone Randall knew, but she had always been too soft in Commander Nicholas Laster's eyes.

Too much like their mother.

Randall shook those thoughts away as he peeked into the infirmary; the lights were dimmed, and all was quiet within. He turned toward the cabins — once the quarters of the Facility's crew, now home to the few humans who lived here — and resumed his walk.

The prixxir chirruped and poked the tip of its snout out of the water, little nostrils flaring.

Sighing, Randall shook his head. Maybe this was a belated acknowledgment of his days as a ranger being over, a subconscious effort to move on.

The betrayal he'd suffered at the hands of his fellow rangers should've been the best indication. Men he'd known for his entire life, who he'd hunted with since he was old enough to lift a firearm, had attempted to relieve Randall from command through use of deadly force. He'd always butted heads with Cyrus Taylor, who'd been a close friend of Randall's father, but how had those disagreements in method escalated into attempted murder?

The main directive of the rangers had been simple — protect the colonists from whatever came. Had that always meant something inhuman was the enemy? Had it always meant destroying things before understanding them?

Had Randall always been so damned naïve?

By the time Randall reached Aymee and Arkon's den, his left shoulder ached. He'd taken a stray bullet there when he'd first confronted the couple on the beach, two months ago, when Cyrus attacked Aymee and the weapon in her hand accidentally discharged. The bastard might as well have shot Randall twice himself.

He shifted the container to his right arm. The prixxir wobbled in the sloshing water and made another of its little sounds as Randall stepped in front of the door, which was cracked open about ten centimeters, and knocked on the doorframe.

Cloth rustled inside, followed by a shriek of laughter and footsteps. The door slid open to reveal Aymee. She wore a broad grin, her curly hair wild around her shoulders.

"Randall! Hi!" Aymee's happiness shone in her brown eyes.

Arkon slipped a tentacle around Aymee's waist and settled a hand on her shoulder as he came up behind her. He regarded Randall with narrowed eyes. Though he was leaner than most of the male kraken Randall had seen, he still towered over most humans; he had to be at least two and a half meters long from the top of his head to the tips of his tentacles. With pointed teeth and wicked claws thrown in for good measure, Arkon looked every bit an apex predator.

Randall couldn't fault the kraken for his jealousy or possessiveness — whatever tension existed between he and Arkon was warranted. Their history, however brief, hadn't exactly been conducive to building trust and friendship.

"Hi, Aymee. I don't want to bother you, but I was hoping you could help me with something," Randall said.

"You're not bothering me." She glanced at Arkon — whose expression made it clear *he* was bothered — and gave his tentacle a pat. "Let me talk to Randall, and then we can get back to our *game*."

A bit of the stiffness eased from Arkon's posture. He brushed his thumb along Aymee's neck with a simple intimacy that would've set a jealous fire in Randall's gut only a month ago.

"I will be waiting, quite eagerly," Arkon said. He leaned his head down and kissed Aymee's cheek, lips lingering for several seconds, before moving back into the room.

"You two playing some Blind Man's Bounty?" Randall asked.

Cheeks reddening, Aymee cleared her throat, but her smile didn't fade. "Something like that. So, what can I help you with? Is it your shoulder?"

Randall moved aside as she stepped into the hallway. "No, shoulder's fine as long as I don't overwork it." He took the container in both hands and held it up. "I know you're not an animal doctor, but I was hoping you might be able to help me tend to this critter. His name's Ikaros."

Aymee's brows rose. "A prixxir? Where did you get it?" She reached into the container and gently rubbed Ikaros's snout with the tip of a finger. Ikaros leaned into the attention, closing his eyes.

Randall smiled. He couldn't deny that the little prixxir was cute. "Melaina found it, and I graciously volunteered to take care of it."

"So, Rhea told you to, huh?" Aymee glanced up at him, smirking.

"Actually, she *asked* me to do it. Guess I'm the animal expert around these parts." He lifted a leg to brace the bottom of the container on his thigh and reached into the water, carefully slipping a hand under Ikaros's belly. He lifted the prixxir out of the red-tinted water. "Something tried to make a meal of him. Is there anything we can do?"

Aymee leaned closer and examined the puncture marks. "Let's take him to the infirmary. I can run a scan to see how serious the damage is and get him patched up. Just give me a sec to tell Arkon."

Randall settled Ikaros into the water as Aymee slipped back into her room. Before he removed his hand, Ikaros caught it with his forepaws and clamped his teeth around one of Randall's fingers with surprising gentleness. The prixxir pulled his head back, ran his rough tongue over Randall's skin a few times, and finally released him.

"Let's go get this little guy checked out," Aymee said when she reemerged.

They walked to the infirmary together. It was the most familiar room in the building for Randall, who'd spent his first two weeks in the Facility laid up in one of these beds, receiving daily shots filled with chemicals he couldn't name to speed along his recovery. Being bedridden for all that time had taken a toll on his body, but the hardest part had been watching Arkon recover from more severe wounds in a matter of days.

Aymee walked to the closest bed and placed a folded blanket atop the sheet. "Go ahead and lay him down," she said as she swung the overhead scanner into place.

Randall removed Ikaros from the water. The prixxir clamped onto Randall's hand, trembling in the open air, and didn't let go once he was down.

"Will my hand be in the way?" he asked.

"Just shift it to the side." She activated the scanner. "Okay, little guy, let's see what's going on."

The scanner projected numerous thin beams of light onto Randall's hand and the prixxir within his gentle grasp, revealing intricate webs of blood vessels beneath skin and scale.

As Aymee adjusted the scanner, it displayed more of the underlying anatomy. The damage to the muscles of the prixxir's hindquarters was apparent, but the nearby bones looked undamaged.

Ikaros made a whining sound and dug his claws into Randall's skin.

Randall shifted his finger to pet the underside of Ikaros's jaw. The prixxir angled his head to close his mouth over Randall's fingertip again, gnawing softly. Was he doing that to comfort himself?

Aymee switched off the scanner and pushed it away. Leaning down, she ran a hand along his scaled back. "Nothing serious. I can clean and seal the wounds, and he'll be good as new in no time."

"Will it hurt him?"

"I can apply an anesthetic around the wounds to numb the surrounding area. That should help. I don't want to risk injecting him in case he has an adverse reaction."

"All right. Let's do it."

Randall held the prixxir in place as Aymee worked. Ikaros clenched his jaw, his little claws and teeth biting into Randall's skin. Randall got the sense that, despite being wounded and frightened, the prixxir was trying to keep from doing him harm.

After she'd sealed the wounds, Aymee wrapped a bandage around the newly healed skin and looked at Randall. "Try to keep him from scratching or biting the area for a day or two to make sure he doesn't open those back up."

"I'll do what I can." Randall lifted Ikaros off the bed and gently pried his hand out of the prixxir's hold. Tiny beads of blood welled where his skin had been broken.

"We should probably get those cleaned up, too."

"It's nothing to fuss over, Aymee."

"I'm not fussing. However small, those were made by a wild

animal. Do you really want to chance an infection?" Aymee's expression communicated her stance clearly — *argue with me at your own risk.*

Ikaros settled himself along Randall's forearm, leaning his chin into Randall's gently rubbing fingers.

Randall placed his free hand atop Aymee's rolling cart.

"How are you doing, Randall?" she asked as she disinfected the little punctures.

"I'm alive," he replied, and then hesitated. She didn't need to be burdened by his troubles, but everything felt so complicated, so confusing. His life spent on the hunt hadn't been easy, but at least it had been straightforward. This was all new territory for him. "I guess I feel...lost, though. Trapped. And part of me feels like I should've died a couple times over by now."

"I'm glad you didn't," she said, setting the disinfectant aside. "I know this isn't what you planned for, or what you wanted, but think of it as a new start. You've earned the trust of some of the kraken, and that goes a long way. You have a place here, Randall, you just need to figure out what you want it to be."

"Easier said than done, I guess. How did you deal with giving everything up? How'd you just leave your old life and accept this one?"

"Because I have hope." Aymee stared at Ikaros silently for a moment. "It might be wishful thinking, but I hope, someday, kraken and humans will come together peacefully. I'd like to go back home. I enjoy my time here, but I miss the sun, I miss land, and most of all, I miss my family. I think I put a lot of stress on my father, too. He's the only doctor in The Watch, and it's all on his shoulders now that I'm gone." She met Randall's gaze. "But if I have to choose, I'll always pick Arkon. Does that make me selfish?"

The question was harder to answer than Randall might've thought. Most everyone he'd talked to in The Watch had said Aymee was a kind woman, always willing to help in whatever way she could. What did it mean that she'd chosen Arkon over everyone and everything she'd known? What was it like to have someone so devoted that they'd give up *everything* for you?

"If it does, it's the best reason for selfishness I can think of," he finally replied.

"That's good to hear," Aymee said with a smile. "I better get back to Arkon." She petted Ikaros before placing her hand over Randall's. "It might not feel like it, but you're not alone here, Randall."

"That's good to hear, too."

Once she'd left, he shifted his attention to Ikaros. The prixxir glanced up at him with half-lidded eyes.

"Let's get you some food," Randall said.

Oddly, his mind drifted to Rhea as he walked to the mess hall; she'd barely left his side during his recovery, and he'd even woken on several occasions to find her leaning on the bed, asleep.

Perhaps Aymee was correct. He *wasn't* alone.

But was that what he wanted?

# CHAPTER 3

"*I*t's been two days. Do you think Ikaros remembers me?" Melaina asked, bouncing with excitement as she and her mother moved along the corridor.

Rhea smiled at the youngling. "Perhaps."

Melaina had begged ceaselessly to visit the creature over those two days. Rhea had been tempted to give in — though it wasn't the prixxir she wanted to see — but she knew the creature needed time to heal and adjust to its new environment.

They passed door after door on their way through the cabins. They'd come often to visit Macy and her youngling, Sarina, but this was their first time going to Randall's room. Rhea's hearts thumped as they reached his door. A strange anxiousness tightened her chest at the prospect of seeing him again, this time in his den.

Before humans came to the Facility, kraken rarely went to one another's dens unless they were mating.

Melaina moved in front of her mother and raised her fist. She knocked rapidly on the door, tentacles shifting restlessly beneath her.

After several moments — each of which felt impossibly long — the door slid open. Randall stood in the doorway, his eyes wide and lips parted as he looked from Rhea to Melaina and back again.

Rhea skimmed her gaze over Randall's half-naked body. Since leaving the infirmary, he'd kept himself fully covered, usually in form-fitting jumpsuits. Now, he wore only pants, leaving his torso bare. His shoulders rose and fell with his heavy breaths and a sheen of sweat coated his skin. Rhea's nostrils flared as she inhaled his masculine scent.

"Can I see Ikaros?" Melaina asked.

Broken from her distraction by her daughter's voice, Rhea lifted her eyes to Randall's.

"Yeah," he said, seeming to shake off his own stupor. "He's roaming around some—" Randall glanced down as the prixxir, limping slightly, walked between his legs and brushed its long, flat tail over his ankle. "He's right here, apparently. There's some food over on the desk if you want to feed him."

"I do! Thank you!" Melaina bent down and wrapped her arms around the creature, cuddling it to her chest as she straightened. She closed her eyes and brushed her cheek against Ikaros's head. Offering Randall a smile, she slipped past him and into his room.

"The creature appears gentle," Rhea said.

Randall twisted to glance over his shoulder. "Ikaros is young. I'm no expert on prixxir, but I don't think he's more than a couple months old. He'd still be with his parents right now, under normal circumstances, so I guess I'm taking their place."

"And he is well?"

"He's not at a hundred percent yet, but he can move around

well enough, and I swear he eats twice his body weight in fish every day."

Rhea smirked. "As do all younglings."

"I guess now I understand why my father used to say he could barely keep enough food in the house while I was growing up." He looked down at his bare chest. "If you give me a minute, I'll go get cleaned up. I didn't expect anyone to stop by."

Her gaze dipped to his body again, and her smirk faded. She took in the contours of his musculature, followed the patch of dark hair on his chest as it flowed toward his waistband, narrowing in its descent. Her fingers twitched with the memory of how his hair had felt beneath her palm.

"I do not mind," she said.

He chuckled, running a hand over his head. "That makes sense."

Rhea raised a brow. "In what way?"

"I haven't seen a kraken with clothes on yet, and I've been here for weeks. I get the sense that nudity doesn't really bother you."

"Why would we wear such constrictive things? They would hinder our swimming and obscure our camouflage."

"When you put it that way, it makes sense. But here I am, talking about your—" his eyes dipped to her chest and rose quickly. He cleared his throat. "I'm sorry, Rhea. I didn't mean to keep you standing in the hallway. Would you like to come in?" He stepped aside and gestured to the room behind him.

Rhea moved through the doorway. Randall's unique scent permeated the air; she inhaled deeply and studied his living space. The prixxir stood atop the desk, gobbling up the flakes of cooked, white meat Melaina was feeding it. The bed, positioned against the wall to the right, was neatly made, something she'd rarely seen in Macy's room. There were a few pieces of clothing visible, but the ones on the table were folded and the shirt on the bed was spread flat.

Had Randall always been so tidy, or was this him taking some control over his life after everything had been turned upside-down?

"He is eating so well," Melaina said, twisting to grin at Rhea and Randall. Her attention immediately swung back to the prixxir. She offered another bite of fish, and the creature devoured the morsel, long tail waving eagerly.

"That's good. It'll help him heal faster," Randall said.

Rhea watched her daughter pet the creature. Melaina's face was aglow with delight, and her eyes sparkled with adoration. Rhea's chest tightened; the youngling's wanderlust had caused trouble over the last year, but seeing Melaina so happy filled Rhea's hearts near to bursting.

And it was because of Randall. He'd made it possible by agreeing to care for the prixxir.

Ikaros chirruped, cocking its head and tilting it back when Melaina dangled a bit of fish higher up. The prixxir followed the moving food with large eyes, and the instant the meat came within its reach, it darted up to snatch the food out of Melaina's fingers. She giggled.

"Once he's fully grown, you won't be able to hold food out of his reach anymore," Randall said. "Not until you grow up, yourself."

"When I'm as tall as you?" Melaina asked.

Randall glanced at Rhea, sweeping his gaze over her from tentacles to head, before looking back at Melaina. "You'll probably be taller than me when you're done."

"Are you done growing? You don't seem so tall for a male."

Rhea smirked.

"Yeah, I'm all done growing. Maybe I'm not as big as Dracchus—"

"*No one* is as big as Dracchus," Melaina interrupted.

Randall smiled. "But I make up for it by being the hairiest one in this whole place."

Melaina laughed, pointing at Randall's chest. "You are!"

"Everyone has to have something they're good at."

"Being the hairiest cannot be all you are good at," Rhea said.

"I might have a few other talents," he replied, eyes roving over Rhea's body again. Her brows rose, and her lips curved into a smile. "But I usually let other people judge that for themselves."

Rhea turned her face toward her daughter. "Melaina, go visit with Macy and Sarina."

Melaina straightened excitedly. "Can I bring Ikaros to show Macy?"

"Maybe another time, kid. He's still adjusting to living in here, and we don't want to overwhelm him," Randall said.

She visibly deflated, but said, "I understand." Melaina turned back to the prixxir and smiled, running her palm along its back. "I will see you again soon, Ikaros."

Randall walked to the desk and knelt. Melaina gently lifted Ikaros and passed him to Randall, giving the creature one more scratch under the chin.

"You can come visit him any time your mom says you can," Randall said, "but you have to promise me you'll check her first."

"I will," Melaina said, her smile widening. She placed a hand on Randall's cheek. "Thank you, Randall."

He smiled back at her, and though his expression was a bit off-balance — perhaps he hadn't anticipated such contact — it was warm and genuine. "Any time. Better go and check on Macy and Sarina now, and make sure they're doing okay."

Melaina hurried to the door, opened it, and left. Rhea placed her hands on the doorframe and leaned into the hallway for a moment, ensuring the youngling went in the correct direction, before glancing at Randall over his shoulder.

He brushed his hand over Ikaros's back much like Melaina had before setting the creature on the floor. "Thanks for stopping by, Rhea. It means a lot to me."

Rhea pressed the button on the wall, closing the door, and turned to face him. There was no reason to hold back; she shifted her skin to a deep maroon and stalked closer to him. She raked her gaze over his body, admiring his strength — so different from that of male kraken, but no less appealing.

Confusion spread over his features, furrowing his brow and tugging his lips into a frown. "Rhea... What's going on?"

She smiled as she approached him and stretched a tentacle to coil around his waist. Her suction cups kissed his bare flesh, sampling the saltiness of his sweat and the sweetness of his skin. She ran the tip of another tentacle over the leg of his pants, wishing they were gone.

Rhea waved her hand toward her pelvis and opened her slit, allowing it to flower for him. "I wish to mate with you, human."

His color changed in the subtle way Macy's and Aymee's sometimes did, face taking on a pinkish hue, and his eyes gleamed as he stared at her slit. "Rhea, I..." Shaking his head, he stepped back, moving his hands to the tentacle around his waist. "It's a bit fast, don't you think?"

She tugged him closer, brushing the backs of her fingers across his temple, teasing herself with a fleeting feel of his soft hair. "We can mate slowly, if you wish."

He released a shuddering breath, fingers tensing on her tentacle, and the heat of his body increased. Clenching his jaw, he took hold of her wrist and guided her arm down while gently pushing her tentacle away with his other hand. "That's not what I mean, Rhea. This whole thing is too fast."

Rhea drew back, skin reverting to its normal gray. She glanced at her wrist, encased within his fingers, and lowered her brow. "You are rejecting me?"

"No, I'm not rejecting you."

"Then you wish to mate?"

"No." He caught his lower lip between his teeth, and that ravenous light flashed in his eyes again. "I mean, not *now*."

Rhea frowned, uncoiling her tentacle from his waist and pulling it away.

Randall released her wrist and ran his hand through his hair, down the back of his head, and around to rub the stubble on his cheek. "This is just...a little more complicated where I'm from. People have sex outside relationships, yeah, but for the most part, it's...a process. Something you build up to."

"I do not understand. If we both wish to mate, why," she waved her hand as she searched for the words, "*build up?*"

"Because mating right now wouldn't be anything more than... lust. A fling."

What was a *fling*? "This has always been the way of the kraken."

He extended his arms to either side, muscles shifting beneath his skin. "I'm not a kraken, Rhea."

She turned her head toward the door. Macy and Aymee were likely in their rooms nearby, two humans who'd brought change to the kraken. Was this part of that change? Had the human females *built up* to something more meaningful with Jax and Arkon?

Rhea was one of the most sought-after females in the Facility. She needed only to look at a male, and he would come, offering his protection, his kills, and his body for her needs. Yet Randall had denied her. *Her.*

She felt out of her element.

"What would you have me do?" Rhea asked.

"Take your time. Show me who you are, and learn who I am."

Rhea frowned and held her hands out to either side, as he had before. "This is me."

"That's what you are, but not *who* you are. I have an idea, but I want to know more." He took her hands in his and held them between their bodies, bridging the space that separated them. His hands were so different — larger than hers, with blunt nails, rough skin, and no webbing between their fingers. "I want to know you better. And, maybe, I'll figure out my place here in the process."

Rhea pulled her hands from his grip and nodded once. "So be it."

His brows rose. "You're not rejecting *me* now, are you?"

She tilted her head. "No, human. We will attempt your ways, but make no mistake—" she leaned closer, leveling her eyes with his, and touched the underside of his chin with the tip of a tentacle "—you are *mine*."

Rhea would shred *any* kraken, male or female, who dared to touch what she considered hers. And this human belonged to her alone.

Randall's eyes widened, and he chuckled. "Damn. Guess you don't mince words, do you?"

Her gaze dipped to his lips, and she was tempted to discover what a *kiss* felt like. "I do not know many of your words."

"Words aren't of much importance, compared to actions," he

said. "You claimed me from the moment they brought me into the infirmary, didn't you?"

She placed a hand on his chest and slowly slid it down his abdomen toward his pelvis. The hair beneath her palm was soft over his hard muscle. Rhea recalled the first time she saw him, recalled her surprise when she'd lifted his blanket to see his cock on full display as he lay in the infirmary bed. She'd been intrigued, curious, and shocked by her immediate attraction to him.

The outline of his hardening shaft was visible through his pants. She smiled and met his gaze again. "I did."

He cleared his throat and caught her wrist again, guiding her hand away from his pelvis. "*Slowly*," he rasped. Lifting her hand, he pressed his lips to her knuckles. Her eyes flared. "Humans have some old sayings. *Patience is a virtue. Good things come to those who wait.* Give this some time, Rhea."

She frowned, searching his face, uncertain of what to do, of what to say. This wasn't how she'd been taught, wasn't how the kraken did things.

"You're interested in me? You want me?" he asked.

"Yes," she replied without hesitation.

"Then shouldn't I be worth some time and effort?" He smiled lopsidedly, and the expression heated her blood.

Rhea drew back. "You want *me* to woo *you*?"

"I just want us to know each other before we jump into each other's pants."

She glanced down at her lower half, confused by his words once again.

"It's an expression," he said. "I mean before we have sex."

"Ah."

"Just give it time. Visit tomorrow with Melaina. Let me get to know you both, and we can move on from there."

She searched his expression. He sounded earnest, but this situation was unfamiliar to her. Did he not want her as much as she wanted him? His body suggested he desired her, even if his words implied otherwise.

What would the other females think of her if they knew she was almost begging a male to mate with her? A human male, no less, when there were several kraken males she could choose from at any moment.

She finally nodded; the opinions of the other females were meaningless. "We will come tomorrow."

Randall released her hand and stepped back, offering a nod of his own. "Good. I look forward to seeing you again."

# CHAPTER 4

*R*andall laid another fillet atop the flat grill. The meat sizzled, its scent adding to the already mouthwatering aroma of cooking fish. A pot of Halorian lobsters boiled on the stovetop nearby, its steam billowing into the automatic fan overhead.

"This is going to be some good eating, little guy," he said.

Ikaros chirruped from his perch atop the counter. The prixxir lifted a paw and waved it toward the food.

Grinning, Randall turned to the island counter behind him and sliced a small piece from one of the remaining raw fillets. He tossed the morsel to Ikaros. The prixxir reared back on his hind legs — his limp was all but gone — and caught the meat in his mouth.

"Maybe I shouldn't let Melaina feed you quite so much. I swear you've gained four kilos since she brought you in."

The prixxir lowered his head, dropped the meat onto the countertop, and gnawed at it.

"Good thing we're not back at Fort Culver. The only animals

allowed on the counters there are the ones that're about to be cooked."

Randall smiled and tended the cooking food as Ikaros ate. He couldn't deny his excitement. For the first time in the weeks he'd spent in the Facility, he was enjoying himself. That was strange after feeling lost and directionless for so long.

Ikaros played a large role in that. The prixxir hadn't left Randall's side since being rescued by Melaina a week before. Though Randall couldn't explain the bond he was forming with the creature, he knew it was powerful. At night, Ikaros curled up against him in bed, and had taken to laying over Randall's feet whenever he was sitting.

The creature had given Randall companionship, *purpose*, and made him feel needed. He'd never reflected upon the importance of such things before — he'd had the other rangers, the directive, the hunt; it had been more than enough to keep him distracted. He hadn't realized how quickly an individual could lose their drive, how quickly a life could lose meaning.

Ikaros had, after only seven short days, become one of Randall's truest and closest friends.

Randall's sister, Elle, had always filled that role before. Thinking about her now made his chest ache; they'd cooked so many meals together, sometimes getting so caught up in conversation that the food would end up a charred mess. She'd been the only one he could ever confide in. And he hadn't seen her in months.

He checked the time on the wall display. Rhea and Melaina would arrive soon; after they'd visited him in his quarters for four consecutive days, he'd decided a change of scenery would be nice, and had invited them to join him in the mess hall for a meal. He wasn't sure what he'd found more endearing — Melaina's excitement at the prospect of eating cooked food, like she sometimes did with Macy, or Rhea's almost comical reluctance. The kraken had eaten everything raw before Macy's arrival, and only Jax, Arkon, and Melaina had been willing to sample cooked meat thus far.

His growing appreciation of Rhea's company was the other component to his change in mood and the reason for his current eagerness. She presented a hard, no-nonsense exterior that would have been welcomed amongst Fort Culver's rangers, but her personality didn't stop there — the kindness and compassion beneath her outer toughness were staggering.

After tossing another chunk of fish to Ikaros, Randall seasoned the fillets with a few pinches of the spices Aymee had sent to Macy from The Watch, careful not to use too much — there was a limited supply, and he wasn't sure how Rhea and Melaina would react to their taste.

Rhea's advances had been so strong and forward that Randall had been taken aback by them, caught totally off-guard and unprepared. It had been a direct confrontation with the strangeness of his situation and the otherness of the kraken.

Randall was attracted to Rhea. There was no denying that fact, especially after she'd seen the evidence with her own eyes. The silky touch of her hand on his abdomen had nearly sent him over the edge, and only his own confusion had held him back; was it *right* to want her? To give in to those urges? To his father, such would be considered bestiality at best, a betrayal of humanity, a violation of natural law.

But the more he learned about her, the more he saw her, the less alien she seemed. The kraken were part human, and their human qualities became more evident to him as time passed. Rhea's differences — cast in the light of her compassion, of her resilience, of her confidence — were marks of beauty unlike any he'd ever encountered.

Was he even capable of pleasing her? Her anatomy, though similar in its basic form to a human woman's, was still different, and Randall wasn't built like a kraken male.

More than anything, he needed to know that their *mating* wasn't merely a matter of Rhea sating her curiosity. From the little he understood about kraken culture, the females chose males based on their ability to protect and provide.

Randall hadn't proven himself a capable provider. They all sure as hell knew he couldn't stand against any of the kraken in a physical confrontation, and he'd never even seen the monstrous sea creatures the kraken sometimes spoke of battling in the open water. He hadn't given her any reason to choose him; being different, being human, couldn't be enough.

And he needed to know that it wouldn't just be an exploration of curiosity on his end, either. He needed to know his interest in her was more than a fleeting lust for the exotic.

Ikaros stood up and spun around, looking through the wide, open window between the kitchen and the mess hall. An instant later, Randall heard the sound of tentacles moving over the floor — usually soft and subtle, but quite distinct from the Facility's ambient sounds.

"I'm in here," Randall called, scooping the finished fillets onto a tray.

At the edge of Randall's vision, Ikaros lowered his stance, swept back his long whiskers, and released a warbling growl. He'd never heard the prixxir make such a sound; the hairs on his arms and the back of his neck stood.

Randall turned to the window to see Kronus — the most vocal of the anti-human kraken — approaching with a pair of his followers. The ochre-skinned kraken scowled at the table Randall had unfolded and placed near the kitchen, shoving it aside as easily as he might've tossed a pebble into a river.

These were the kraken who most resisted change. Who resented it.

The trio moved toward the entryway into the kitchen. Ikaros's growl deepened, and the prixxir retreated closer to the edge of the counter.

"That's close enough," Randall said, dropping a hand to the pistol on his hip.

Kronus stopped and glared at Randall through the window, skin taking on a crimson tinge. "You do not give me orders, *human.*"

When Rhea said *human*, it was an endearment. From Kronus's mouth it was filthy, derogatory, and brimming with malevolence.

Randall unfastened the holster's retaining strap and wrapped his fingers around the pistol's grip. Kronus wasn't the biggest of his kind, or the strongest, but Randall had seen the kraken's capabilities. Even with a half-wall and three or four meters of distance between himself and Kronus, the danger was immediate.

If the kraken got anywhere within reach, Randall would be dead in a fraction of a second.

"It's not an order. Just a warning," he said.

"Shoot, human," one of the others said, lips spread into a wide, razor-sharp grin. "It will only give us reason to tear you apart."

"You stay where you are, and I won't have any reason. But if you have other plans...you'd best ask yourselves if you're willing to die today. Because I guarantee, one of you will be dead before the other two get here." Randall slid the firearm from the holster but kept the barrel pointed down. His heart thumped. It wasn't fear; this was the beginning of an adrenaline high. "If you have business with me, I'm more than willing to talk. I'm sure we can all keep it friendly."

A brown kraken broke away from the group and moved to the open doorway, filling the space with his muscular frame. He ducked as though to enter the kitchen.

Ikaros leapt to the floor, raising his spine fin and whiskers and growling beside Randall's feet.

Randall picked up a knife off the table with his free hand and threw it without hesitation. It embedded itself in the doorframe, centimeters from the brown kraken's head.

Snarling, the kraken bared his teeth and lifted his claws, skin turning red. "The human struck first."

Kronus crossed his arms over his chest. "We have borne witness to this attack."

"You've witnessed a second warning," Randall said. "If I'd attacked, his brains would be splattered on the floor behind him. I'll say this one more time: if you have business with me, I'm willing to talk, but you're going to back the hell up first."

The brown kraken lunged forward. Time seemed to slow as Randall raised his pistol. He wished he hadn't experienced moments like this so often over the last few months, wished that he wasn't staring his own death in the eyes once again, especially now that he'd found a new reason to live.

A tentacle wrapped around the kraken's throat from behind. His upper body pivoted backwards, at odds with the forward momentum of his lower half, and then he was swung around and shoved away from the entrance, sprawling onto his back.

Rhea imposed herself in the doorway with her back turned to Randall. Her skin was a vibrant red, and her face was in profile as she glared at Kronus and the other kraken.

Tentacles writhing, the brown kraken flipped himself onto his front, pushed up on his hands, and bared his teeth at Rhea.

"You have defied myself and Dracchus again," she said.

"Your pet human attacked without provocation," Kronus growled.

"Krullshit," Randall said. "I gave you clear boundaries, and you chose to cross them. Can't blame me for your inability to follow simple instructions."

Rhea turned her head toward the brown kraken, who was lifting himself off the floor. "Is this true, Neo?"

Neo rubbed his throat before pointing toward the doorway. "We are not restricted from entering a room!"

Rhea stared at Neo. "What need have you to enter this room? Were you intending to cook your next meal?" She looked between the three of them. "I see no food."

"The humans have begun corrupting our females, as well," Neo spat. "Beware, Rhea. Your slit will not protect you from retribution now that you have chosen to betray our people along with the others."

Rhea narrowed her eyes and advanced toward Neo. "You dare speak to me so?"

Neo's brows fell, and his jaw muscles bulged. He was larger and undoubtedly stronger than Rhea, but kraken society valued the females — precious few in number — over the males. When it came to her, his threats were all bluster, and he knew it.

Randall shifted his pistol, training it on the other two kraken through the window; his fascination with the confrontation couldn't be allowed to hinder his awareness.

The male beside Kronus moved forward slowly, inserting himself between Neo and Rhea. His tan skin turned yellow as he bowed his head.

"Apologies, Rhea," he said. "We were curious about what the human was doing. Neo wanted to look closer, but the human threw a knife at him." He raised his head and shifted closer to Rhea, brushing the back of his fingers down her arm. The yellow of his skin gave way to maroon. "I would make a good protector for you and Melaina. My den is empty, and I will gladly share it with you."

Rhea's skin reverted to its usual gray.

The nuances of kraken social interaction were mysterious to Randall; he didn't understand how the conversation had taken such a sudden, unexpected turn. But he did understand the twisting, forceful weight in his gut, and the fire in his chest. This wasn't about the implication that he'd make a poor mate, though that stung on its own. No, this was about someone attempting to take Rhea. To seduce her.

"She already claimed her male," Randall said, approaching the doorway, "and it sure as hell isn't you."

The male in front of Rhea laughed. "You are not strong enough to protect this female and her youngling." His hands settled on Rhea's hips. "You cannot please a female, and you cannot even dance as we do. You are *weak*." Two of his front tentacles lifted to brush along Rhea's.

"Maybe not." Randall stepped through the doorway into the mess hall, aiming the pistol at the kraken in front of Rhea. "But she claimed me anyway. And I'm a damned good shot, if nothing else. Keep your hands on my female if you want to find out just how good."

The male growled.

Kronus moved forward. "You cannot claim our females!"

"You might not have noticed, but we humans do things a little differently."

The nearness of the male kraken should've been terrifying, but adrenaline pumped through Randall's veins, fueled by his anger. He'd been given no choice other than to stay in this place, and he was tired of walking on eggshells, tired of being treated like an inferior creature, of being looked at like some disgusting insect. If the kraken understood strength, he'd show it to them in the only ways he could.

"Rhea?" asked the male holding her.

Rhea grinned, her blue eyes bright with mirth and pride. "You heard the same words as I, Volk. The human belongs to me, and he has claimed me in turn."

Volk's skin flashed red, then violet before he abruptly released her and backed away. He clenched his jaw and fisted his hands at his sides.

Rhea moved behind Randall, settling her hands on his waist and running a tentacle up and down his leg. His heart beat faster, and his skin tingled at her touch.

She leaned forward and pressed her cheek against his. "I have made my choice. Now, must I remind you again that these humans are under protection? I will not take kindly to you threatening them further. Nor will Dracchus, Jax, and Arkon."

Behind Randall, the prixxir growled. Randall shifted his gaze to see Neo, eyes locked on Ikaros, approaching slowly.

"The prixxir is under *my* protection," Randall said. "Don't touch him."

Neo glared at Randall. He cast one more look at the prixxir and moved toward Kronus, but not before spitting at Rhea's tentacles.

Rhea flared red and lunged toward Neo, but Randall wrapped an arm around her. Her strength and momentum nearly dragged him off-balance, yet he somehow held on and brought her to a halt. He tugged her against him.

Kronus narrowed his eyes. "I am not sure which of you is the other's keeper, but it is pathetic either way."

"No one will want a slit contaminated by human seed," Neo added.

The male kraken turned away and exited the mess hall, casting numerous scowling glares over their shoulders as they moved.

Rhea snarled and threw herself at the male kraken again, but Randall held her firm, gritting his teeth against the strain. His shoulder screamed in protest of the harsh treatment. He hoped she didn't have any more strength in reserve, or he'd quickly lose the struggle.

When the males were out of sight, she finally settled, still save for her heavy breathing. Anger pulsed from her in waves.

Soon, her breathing steadied and her skin reverted to normal. Randall slowly eased his hold on her. He realized only then that one of his hands cupped her breast. It was small and firm, but yielded to his fingers, her nipple hard against his palm. Her scent wafted over him; crisp, salt-kissed wind and rain.

Desire flooded Randall, and his cock hardened. It took all his willpower to keep from squeezing her breast, from stroking her nipple, from turning her around to discover its taste with his tongue.

"It was my right to punish them," Rhea said, though her voice held less command than usual.

"Punish them for what? Being dickheads?" Randall shook his head, trying — and failing — to ignore the new tone in her voice, the heat of her skin, the way her body felt against his. "They're not worth the trouble."

One of her tentacles ran up his leg as Ikaros chirruped behind him.

Randall released her abruptly and stepped back, ending the dangerous contact. He ran his tongue over suddenly dry lips. "Thanks for the assist, by the way. You're the only reason they stopped."

"Hmm," was her only reply as she turned toward Ikaros. The prixxir stood near the folded tables in the corner. "Melaina, come."

The little girl peeked out from behind one of the tables. She smiled at Randall before emerging fully from her hiding place, bending down to scoop Ikaros into her arms.

Rhea looked at Randall, her blue eyes bright. "We have come for the meal my male said he would provide us."

Her words instilled in him a strange mixture of pride and shame; under different circumstances, he wouldn't have simply cooked the food for them, he'd have been the one to hunt it, kill it, clean and butcher it. He would have truly provided for Rhea, Melaina, and Ikaros. Despite his inability to do so, she'd stood up for him, had leapt to his defense, had *chosen* him. Rhea had been openly hostile with some of her own people because of him.

That had to be more than curiosity. She actually wanted *him*.

*And I want* her.

But he had to prove himself worthy, first. Had to earn her.

He *would* earn her.

# CHAPTER 5

*R*hea lazily stroked the bare skin of Randall's ankle with a tentacle as she sat nestled between his legs. The steady thump of his heart pulsed through her back, and she leaned into it. She ran her fingers over the blanket spread on the floor beneath them and turned her attention toward her daughter.

Melaina was asleep on the bed with an arm curled around Ikaros. The gentle breaths of youngling and prixxir were the only sounds in the quiet room, accented by the occasional soft chirrup from Ikaros.

Today had been a good day. A *wonderful* day, despite the earlier encounter with Kronus and his followers. Rhea had never felt so content in all her years, save in the moment of Melaina's birth.

After eating the meal Randall had prepared, they'd explored the Facility, taking him to some of the rooms he hadn't seen. Melaina had darted along the hallways with Ikaros in pursuit, filling the space with her joy and laughter.

*And I have tried to stifle that joy.*

Rhea's own prejudice against the humans had driven her to

threaten Macy the first time they met, hoping it would keep her daughter away from the woman. But in the time since, she'd developed a deep friendship with Macy, and Melaina loved spending time with the humans. Rather than being adversely affected by contact with Macy, Aymee, and Randall, Melaina had been enriched.

"What are you thinking?" Randall asked, his breath a warm caress on the back of her neck.

"My daughter is happy."

"Wasn't she before?"

"Not before you and Macy." Rhea frowned. "Kraken live alone. We keep to ourselves, to our own dens, and rarely seek one another's company. Melaina was all I had. I was all she had."

"What about her father?"

"Vasil. A good hunter, an attractive male, and my second choice when Jax refused me."

His hold around her stiffened. "He's...still around?"

Rhea leaned forward and twisted her torso to look at him over her shoulder. His brow was creased, his jaw clenched. "Yes. Why?"

"Doesn't he see her?"

"He sees her."

One of his eyebrows rose. "You said that strangely. I don't think we're talking about the same thing. You said you and Melaina were all either of you had. Does he not spend time with her often, or what?"

Before Macy, Rhea likely wouldn't have been able to decipher his meaning on her own. But after seeing Jax and Macy as a family, caring for their youngling *together*, she understood.

"He has never spoken to her. My mating with Vasil was fleeting. He does not know that he sired Melaina," Rhea said. She placed a hand over one of his and continued before he could speak again. "The kraken are not like the humans, Randall. Female kraken take mates at our whims, and when we have not conceived or grow bored, we choose new males. We raise female younglings throughout their lives, but we keep males only until they are old enough to join the hunters. It is rare for a youngling to know who their sire is.

"It was not until Macy brought her human ways that we knew things could be different. Jax found a mate he did not wish to leave, a mate who did not want to leave him. And it has made Melaina happy to be around people who care for her, who enjoy spending time with her. People who love her."

"And what about you, Rhea?" The tips of his fingers trailed lightly over her abdomen, and his eyes seemed a darker blue than usual.

"What about me?"

"Are you happy?"

Rhea turned toward the bed, tracing her daughter's delicate features with her gaze. She smiled. "I am."

Before the humans had come, Rhea's existence had been defined by her daughter — keeping Melaina fed, protecting her from danger, showing her what it meant to be a kraken female, and doing whatever she could think of to discourage the youngling's wanderlust and overwhelming curiosity. But the humans' new perspectives had shown Rhea there could be more. There was room for herself and her daughter to find happiness, even if it meant relinquishing a little control. Melaina would find her way better with gentle guidance than with overbearing protectiveness.

The humans had brought *love* to the kraken.

Rhea knew now that she'd always loved Melaina, since the moment she'd first felt the flutter of life inside herself, but the humans had taught her new ways to express that feeling. New ways to experience it.

Could she and Randall come to share it, one day?

"Good," Randall said. He leaned forward and rested his chin on her shoulder, pressing his cheek against hers. The small hairs on his face scratched her skin, but the sensation wasn't unpleasant. Rather, it sent a tingling thrill through her, and she found herself wanting to feel it on other parts of her body.

She dropped her gaze to his hands, which were settled at her middle. There was a sprinkling of dark hair across their backs, which thickened as it went up his arm. The female humans had hair on their arms, too, though it was shorter, lighter, and harder to notice. Rhea looked at her own hairless arm.

All her life, she'd been trained to be confident, to understand that her place amongst the kraken was one of privilege. She was female. She was rare. She was *important*. Males fought for her attention, for the honor of mating with her. Now, for the first time, Rhea felt unappealing.

It was not a good feeling.

"Do you find me attractive?" she asked.

"Of course I do." Randall's hands slid to her hips, and he guided her to turn around and face him. "I didn't know what to think, at first. You're so different from everything I've known. But every piece of you," he trailed his fingertips along one of her tentacles, over her hand and up her arm, across the sensitive skin of her siphon, "is beautiful."

Rhea brushed her fingers through his hair, admiring its softness, before touching her own bald head. "I will never have hair like your females."

He took her hand in his as she lowered it. "And I will never have tentacles."

She wrapped the end of a tentacle around his wrist. "You do not mind that we are so different?"

Randall smoothed a hand up her shoulder to cup the back of her head. She saw his answer in his gaze a moment before he pulled her close and covered her mouth with his.

Rhea grasped his arms as her eyes fluttered closed. Heat spread through her body, trailing along her limbs, flooding her core. Her tentacle fell from his wrist to encircle his waist, and she leaned closer. He shifted his lips, and she felt the moist touch of his tongue against the seam of her mouth. Her lips parted in surprise. Randall's tongue slid through to brush behind her teeth and stroke her tongue, beckoning it to join his.

This was a kiss. This wild, thrilling act, unknown to the kraken until recently, was a kiss. And it was *glorious*.

She moved her mouth against his, tasted his lips, tasted his tongue, but it wasn't enough. She needed to be closer.

Rhea slid her arms around his neck, pressing her breasts to his chest as the kiss deepened.

Randall dropped a hand to her hip again, sliding it to her back to draw her pelvis against his. He groaned. The sound vibrated through her, making the tips of her tentacles curl in anticipation. His hardness probed her lower belly, signaling his want, and she grazed her claws over his shoulder.

He abruptly broke the contact between their mouths, pulling away. His lips were red, his eyes dark and glowing with passion. Between ragged breaths, he flicked his gaze toward Melaina and Ikaros, who still slept soundly on the bed.

"Believe me when I tell you it's not easy for me to say, Rhea... but we should stop."

Rhea frowned. "I do not understand. You are ready to mate, as am I."

Randall released a sound that was half shaky sigh, half chuckle, and leaned his forehead against hers. "Just give me time, Rhea."

At best, the rules of human relationships were confusing to Rhea; right now, they were outright frustrating. Why wait when they were both willing? Both *wanting*? "I feel the proof of your desire now, human. What time could you possibly need?"

He sat back and shook his head. "For starters, your daughter is two meters away."

She glanced toward Melaina. "She is sleeping."

"And I would rather not be in the middle of it when she wakes up."

"If it is privacy you wish, we can move to the hall."

Randall smirked, but the light in his eyes had already changed. His gaze burned with passion, but not with the immediate, scalding flames that had scorched her only moments ago. "It's selfish of me to hold you to my way of doing things without any consideration for your traditions. If I was just another kraken male competing for your attention, you wouldn't have given me a second look so far. You don't even know if I can provide for you and your kid, or if I can protect you."

She opened her mouth to deny his words, but nothing came out. He was partially right. Randall hadn't done anything to prove his worth as a provider, though he'd demonstrated his ability as a protector by saving Jax from the other humans. But it was his inner strength that had drawn Rhea to him during those first weeks — the strength of his resolve, his unwavering humor in the face of his circumstances, his easy adaptability.

Rhea loosened her hold on Randall but didn't release him. "What is it you wish?"

"Females choose the males, don't they? That's the way of your people?"

"It is."

"I want to be chosen because I'm worthy, not because I'm...exotic."

She tilted her head and searched his face. Perhaps that had been part of his draw, in the beginning — she'd been fascinated by him, the first and only human male she'd ever seen — but it wasn't the sole reason she'd chosen him. "You wish to go slow. To prove yourself to me."

"To you, and to myself." He gripped her chin gently with his forefinger and thumb. "But don't doubt that I want you, because once I prove that I can provide for and protect you and Melaina, you will be *mine*."

Pleasure blossomed in her chest at his words. Before Randall, the thought of a male claiming *her* would have bothered Rhea. Now the thought tantalized her. Perhaps it was because she wanted him more than any male she'd known.

Rhea nodded. "I will give you time, but you must agree to continue kissing me."

A wide smile spread across his lips. "Deal."

# CHAPTER 6

"It does not seem wise to grant your request, Randall," Dracchus said, folding his arms across his chest. His voice was a deep rumble, the sort that always sounded to Randall like it must have pained the speaker.

"I've spent my whole life outside, Dracchus," Randall said. "These walls are driving me crazy. I'm not asking to go to land, just to get out of this building for a little while."

"After you threw a knife at Neo—"

"That was two weeks ago! Are they still complaining about it?"

Dracchus frowned; he probably wasn't interrupted often, and he didn't seem to appreciate it. "They have used it to rally a few more kraken to their cause. Proof of how dangerous humans are."

"They would've torn me apart without a second thought."

"I know. But that does little to change minds that were already made up. Letting you outside, even for a short while, will be viewed as allowing you a chance to escape."

Randall sighed and ran a hand through his hair. It wouldn't be smart to take out his frustration on Dracchus, even verbally, but it was still a struggle to bite his tongue.

The time he'd spent with Rhea had been wonderful over the last two weeks. The confrontation with Kronus, Neo, and Volk had, unexpectedly, brought Randall and Rhea closer together. He still hadn't given in fully, but he'd come to accept his desires. Her understanding of what he'd requested seemed to grow a little every day. She'd even confessed to speaking of it with Macy and Aymee to learn the perspective of the female humans.

Melaina was a joy, too, and Ikaros was more energetic and playful than Randall had thought possible. Kronus and his followers had kept their distance since the incident in the mess hall. Everything considered, life was surprisingly joyful.

But these walls were driving Randall insane.

If he couldn't get fresh air — and holy hell, he *wanted* some fresh air, wanted real wind on his face — he at least needed a change of scenery.

"So, letting me out would be taken as you disrespecting their stance?" Randall asked.

"Yes."

"Isn't that alone worth it to you?"

Dracchus's brows fell low over his piercing amber eyes, and he pressed his lips into a tight line. Ikaros stepped past Randall and sat beside the kraken, swatting at a moving tentacle. Dracchus looked down, frown deepening, and pulled the tentacle away. Ikaros pounced.

Sinking into a crouch, Dracchus slipped a hand beneath the prixxir and lifted him off the floor. The kraken and the prixxir stared into one another's eyes for several seconds. "Your beast is a clumsy hunter."

"He's just playing," Randall replied, just before Dracchus's words sparked a new thought. "You're a hunter."

Dracchus grunted affirmatively.

"I've hunted my entire life, but never underwater, and Ikaros was too young to hunt when he was brought here. Take us out there. Teach us. You accepted me as one of your people, so let me contribute."

The large kraken's gaze shifted from Randall to Ikaros and back again, skepticism and scrutiny written in the set of his mouth and the crease between his brows. "You are unable to hunt in the manner of my people," Dracchus said after a long silence, "and your beast is a youngling still."

Small as Ikaros was, the prixxir had gained at least twenty-five centimeters in three weeks, and his once scrawny frame had filled out. A few more weeks and Ikaros would likely top a meter from his snout to the tip of his tail.

"He should be catching his own small prey by now, and there are plenty of tools in this place that would allow me to get in that water and hunt."

Dracchus set Ikaros down and rose. "So now you wish for me to arm you and let you out into the water?"

Randall threw his arms to the sides. "What do you want me to do, Dracchus? Either I have a place here, or I don't. If you don't give me a chance to earn trust, to prove that I have value, why keep me alive? Give me a chance."

"At what risk to my people?"

"My people, my hunting party, betrayed me. But I was conscious when you first brought me here. I heard what you said to Kronus. You said that we — me, Aymee, and Macy — are your people now, too. If I'm one of you, how is there a risk? Let me earn my place. Take me out there. Watch me like you're guarding a prisoner if you must, as long as I can get out of these walls for a while."

The kraken's siphons flared open and closed as he stared down at Ikaros. The prixxir sat on the floor with surprising patience, tail swishing slowly over the floor, and stared up at Dracchus.

"What if your beast swims away, Randall?"

The thought produced an unexpected pang of sadness in Randall's chest. A few weeks wasn't much time, in the grand scheme, but Ikaros had become such a large part of his life that he couldn't imagine things without the prixxir around.

"If he wants to go, he'll go," Randall replied. "I'm not going to keep him on a leash. I trust him enough to let him choose."

Mild confusion touched Dracchus's features. "You are comparing the situation between you and your beast to the situation between you and I?"

Randall shrugged. "Yeah."

"These situations are different. If the beast leaves, it will not call its kind to attack this place."

"Neither will I."

"How can I trust that?"

"Because there are people in here I care about too much to put them in that kind of danger."

"You want to prove yourself to Rhea."

It stung a bit, hearing his primary motive spoken out loud, but that made it no less true.

No matter how much skill and dedication Randall had displayed, there'd always been rangers who thought he'd been given command of his own team only because his father was the man in charge. Cyrus had been among the most vocal, especially while they were in the field. Randall had never revealed how much it had bothered him because some part of him had suspected they were right.

He wouldn't allow it to be the same with the kraken. This was a fresh start, a chance to earn his place, to succeed or fail based solely on his own capabilities. And he was competing against beings who were physically superior to him in almost every way.

"Yes," he said.

"Do you know what this would mean for you? Kraken females are few. Claiming one for yourself will mean constant competition." Dracchus looked Randall up and down and shook his head. "Even the weakest of our males is more than a match for you."

"Isn't that why you agreed to let me carry this?" Randall patted the holstered pistol on his hip. There'd been a few demands to have it taken away from him after the incident with Kronus, but Dracchus, Jax, and Arkon had overridden them.

"You cannot shoot your way through every confrontation."

"That's almost funny coming from you; Macy told me how you wanted to fight your way into The Watch to rescue Jax."

Dracchus furrowed his brow. "You are comparing two different situations again."

"Yeah. That's totally valid when it comes to comparison."

"Perhaps I should have left Arkon to deal with you. He is better able to understand the way you humans speak."

Randall smirked. "But he doesn't like me as much as you do."

"I have not decided whether I like you or not."

Perhaps it was his imagination, but Randall thought there was a hint of humor in Dracchus's eyes.

"That puts you ahead of Arkon, I'd say."

Dracchus fell silent and lowered his gaze to Ikaros.

Randall concentrated on keeping his expression neutral to hide his anxiety. Dracchus could be reasoned with, but he was what the rangers would've called, with the utmost respect, a hard ass.

"Come with me, human," Dracchus finally said.

Releasing a long, quiet breath, Randall followed Dracchus through corridors that had become maddeningly familiar over the last several weeks. Ikaros's claws clicked on the floor as the prixxir trailed close behind.

The Facility had no shortage of dark, abandoned rooms that no longer served a purpose; they entered one of them, and Randall stopped in front of a desk.

Dracchus rounded the desk and bent down, feeling for something on its underside.

Before Randall could ask what the kraken was doing, a panel on the wall behind the desk slid upward, revealing an alcove a meter wide and two meters tall with three shelves built into it. Diving suits — made of sleek black material that stretched to fit the wearer — were folded neatly along the top, each with an accompanying mask. The lower shelves held piles of weaponry. Harpoon guns, rifles, pistols, heat guns, all stacked haphazardly into a space never intended to house them.

Randall cringed at the sight. Firearms were an integral part of life in Fort Culver, always treated with care and respect. It hurt a little to see this mess, especially when the weapons down here were in near perfect condition; as far as he knew, the only use they might've seen was when the kraken overthrew the humans in the Facility hundreds of years before.

"You are not meant to know of this," Dracchus said, straightening. "I am extending you my trust, Randall. Break it, and I will break you."

Coming from a creature that had to be well over three meters long if he lay down and weighed more than four hundred kilograms, it was no idle threat.

"You'll have to get in line for that, Dracchus." Randall stepped toward the alcove and looked over the weaponry with wonder. There were several models of firearms that he'd only heard about through historical holos, and he'd never held anything that was in such good condition. Everything the rangers possessed had been passed down from generation to generation, repaired and rebuilt with whatever parts and methods were available as years passed and the colonization became history.

A chirrup from behind caught Randall's attention. He turned to the desk to see Ikaros atop it. The prixxir walked to the edge nearest Dracchus and lifted a paw, brushing it lightly over the kraken's tentacle. Dracchus ran his palm over the prixxir's head and back, folding down the little top fin along its spine.

"Suit in and select a harpoon gun. I will meet you at the main entrance," Dracchus said.

"Suit *up*."

Dracchus grunted questioningly.

"It's suit *up*, not suit *in*."

"If you understand what I mean either way, human, what is the issue?"

Randall shrugged as he unzipped his jumpsuit. "Can't really argue your point."

"Hurry, human." With that, Dracchus exited the room. The sound of the kraken's tentacles moving along the corridor floor gradually faded.

After stripping out of his clothes, Randall donned a PDS — personal diving suit — and lifted the mask, which appeared to be little more than a clear piece of glass, into place. The suit automatically sealed the mask to the hood. A faint tingle spread over Randall's skin as the suit's systems came online.

"Hello, Sam," he said.

"Hello, diver seven-seven-four," replied Sam, the suit's internal computer.

Randall selected a harpoon gun and slung it over his shoulder before making his way toward the building's main entrance.

He grew accustomed to the feel of the suit as he walked. He'd only worn such a suit once — when he was brought to the Facility. His injuries, paired with the overwhelming nature of the situation that had seen him in the suit to begin with, had proven too distracting for him to learn the feel and functions of the PDS that first time.

Ikaros brushed his side along Randall's leg on a few occasions during the journey, releasing uncertain chirrups as he did so. Randall felt the slight pressure against his calf, but the sensation was different, distant, more a suggestion of a feeling than the real thing.

Dracchus awaited at the door to the pressurization chamber. "Do you know our signals, human?"

Though the audio was high quality, there was something about the way the suit relayed sound that was off. It seemed more pronounced with Dracchus's voice. Perhaps it was the kraken's deep bass, or simply the age of the device.

"No, they're quite a bit more complicated than anything I'm familiar with," Randall replied. From what little he'd seen, the kraken had an entire language of gestures involving all their limbs and their ability to change color. It was as similar to the simple hand gestures the rangers used in the field as a log cabin was to a pile of fallen branches.

Dracchus's signature frown returned. "Perhaps it would be best to wait."

"Hell no! We'll figure it out. We're not going far anyway, right?"

"I did not plan to."

"Perfect. No problem, then." Randall stepped closer to the door.

"Do you wish to exit the base?" Sam asked, sounding almost as excited as Randall felt.

"Yes."

Dracchus cast a questioning glance at Randall, but the chamber door slid open before the kraken could voice an inquiry.

The trio moved into the pressurization chamber; Randall first, with Ikaros and Dracchus close behind. They were a collection of beings that shouldn't have had a place together, that shouldn't have found common ground or common purpose.

Randall's heart thumped as the door closed behind them and the room flooded. Ikaros splashed through the water, chirruping happily.

"Remain close at all times," Dracchus said. "We will hunt only fish and bottom feeders, keeping the Facility within view as much as possible."

Randall rounded his lips and released a slow breath. Anticipation thrummed through him, speeding his heartbeat and heating his blood. The water rose past his waist.

Some small part of him wondered why he wasn't planning an escape.

This wasn't his world, these weren't his people. What future could he have down here, really? Half the kraken wanted to kill him and most of the others didn't care if he lived or died.

His sister and father cared, though. How long would it be

before they came looking? If Jon Mason made it back to the fort with news of the kraken's existence, Randall's father would come. And when they discovered Randall was missing...

He didn't want Elle caught up in any of this. He'd nearly lost her once already, long ago, and couldn't bear that pain again. As much as it hurt to think he'd never see her again, at least she was safe at Fort Culver. But if their father brought her here, used her skills against the kraken, she'd be in immense danger.

He cast those worries aside as the water lifted his feet off the floor and he was completely submerged. None of this was easy, none of it was without danger, but when he thought of Rhea, Melaina, Ikaros, and the others, he knew it was worth the risks.

Ikaros darted around Randall, thick tail moving like a paddle to propel the prixxir through the water. Randall smiled, watching the little creature until a green light came on over the exit.

"Pressurization complete," Sam chimed.

Randall slipped the harpoon gun off his shoulder, ensured the safety was engaged, and fastened the loop dangling from its grip around his wrist. He met Dracchus's gaze and the two exchanged a nod. The kraken reached forward and pressed the button on the wall, and the door slid open.

Ikaros bolted into the open water. Randall and Dracchus emerged a moment later, watching the creature zip along. The prixxir used its webbed paws for increased mobility, keeping its legs folded along its belly. Randall didn't know if Ikaros was faster than a kraken, but there was no question of the prixxir being faster than a human, suit or no suit.

As Ikaros swam farther away, his form darkening in the cerulean water, fear gripped Randall's insides. It was one thing to say he'd be fine with Ikaros leaving, but now that the possibility stared him in the face it was impossible to ignore.

The door closed behind them, but Randall was only distantly aware of it, just as he was only distantly aware of Dracchus floating nearby.

Keeping his eyes on Ikaros, Randall swam forward. His limbs moved with surprising ease, as though the water put up no resistance, and each motion propelled him farther than it seemed it should have. He was certain his muscles would eventually ache if only because they were unused to the movements, but even his shoulder felt good for now.

He glanced down. The seafloor below was a mixture of sand, stone, and scattered vegetation, as varied and vibrant as anything on land. His eyes roved over his surroundings, drinking in the details within his limited field of view — on the surface, one could see for kilometers under the right conditions, but down here everything succumbed to the blue haze of unending water looming in all directions. It was at once immense and oppressive.

Something rubbed against his leg. He glanced down to see Ikaros's tail curled around his calf. The prixxir chirruped — the sound was higher and eerier in the relative silence of the ocean — and released its loose hold to swim around Randall in quick circles.

A flash of color to the right caught Randall's attention — Dracchus. The kraken reverted his skin to its normal shade and motioned for Randall to follow.

They moved at an easy pace, keeping a few meters above the bottom, and approached a jutting rockface. Coral and tall, swaying stalks of purple and green seaweed ran along its crest. As they neared the exposed stone, Randall noted tiny creatures moving over it and weaving in and out of its holes and recesses — some looked like fish, others were wormlike or serpentine, and yet more resembled hard-shelled insects.

Dracchus led them up the steep incline, gesturing for Randall to keep near the rock. Ikaros fell into place beside Randall, whiskers twitching and eyes darting from sea creature to sea creature. Somehow, the prixxir remained close, resisting what must've been an instinctual drive to pursue prey.

As they reached the crest, the extent of the vegetation atop it became clear — this wasn't a field of seagrass, but an underwater forest, granting only fleeting glimpses of the larger creatures lurking within. Some of the fish drifting through the stalks appeared to be more than a meter long, though it was impossible to know for sure.

Dracchus slowed to a stop three or four meters from the edge of the seaweed and sank to the sand. Randall lowered himself nearby. Only Ikaros ventured closer, dropping to slither along the bottom on his belly, going so far as to slip the tip of his snout into the vegetation. His whiskers swept forward and brushed along the stalks, and his spine fin rose and fell.

Randall turned to Dracchus. The kraken went through a series of gestures — pointing to his eyes and then the weed, flashing his skin a shade of green just off that of the vegetation, and then indicated Randall's harpoon.

*Watch for something green in the vegetation and shoot?* Randall could only hope that was the kraken's meaning.

Altering his color to match the plants, Dracchus crept forward, drawing himself along with his hands, and vanished into the swaying forest. Randall shifted into a sitting position, leaned back, and swung the harpoon gun into his hands, angling it slightly upward and releasing the safety. He ran his eyes along the seaweed to watch for movement beyond the ordinary. Ikaros moved back and forth along the bottom of Randall's vision, whiskers alert, slow but impatient.

The diving suit transmitted audio from the surrounding water, but it was muted, and Randall couldn't be certain which sounds were normal. His gaze drifted toward the surface high overhead, through which shafts of sparkling light poured to cast restless, web-like shadows on the seafloor. The ocean cradled him, making him feel weightless. All in all, it was a soothing environment, one that wanted to lull him into relaxation and comfort.

And for that, he didn't trust it. The jungle was always at its most dangerous when it was quiet; the ocean's similar quiet set off all his internal alarms.

The first hint that something was approaching came from Ikaros. The prixxir halted his restless swim-walking and raised his head, whiskers flaring. He backed away from the edge of the vegetation with his spine fin raised.

Randall followed Ikaros's gaze with his own and adjusted his hold on the harpoon gun. Something moved within the stalks, and the water displaced by its movement rippled through the seaweed. Whatever this was, it was big. That it might've been Dracchus didn't cross Randall's mind. The big kraken took hunting as seriously as Randall did, and wouldn't pull such a stunt — not even to prove some sort of point.

Inhaling, Randall moved two fingers over the lever that served as the harpoon gun's trigger. His heartbeat quieted, his thoughts stilled, and even the anticipation churning his gut couldn't break his focus.

A sea monster erupted from the seaweed in a torrent of rushing water.

Visual information flooded Randall's mind over a fraction of a second. The creature was easily five meters long, its body shaped like a cylinder with two sides pressed in. Pale scars crisscrossed its mottled purple-and-green hide. Its mouth was on the underside of its wedge-shaped head, a pair of mandibles drawing aside to reveal a ring of jagged, uneven teeth.

Ikaros darted aside, avoiding the charging creature. The thing's mouth looked nasty, but it was disproportionately small compared to its body. A predator, but one that hunted small prey despite its impressive size. Randall recognized the green of its skin as the same color Dracchus had shown him.

Without further thought, Randall aimed the harpoon gun and squeezed the trigger. The gun thumped. The harpoon sped forward amidst a cloud of angry bubbles. Gleaming in the filtered sunlight, the head of the harpoon punched into the creature's mouth and burst out the top of its head.

The creature's body convulsed and thrashed, and it veered to Randall's right. The line connecting the harpoon to the gun went taut. Digging his heels into the sand, Randall held tight. The weight and momentum of the creature threatened to tear his arms out of their sockets, and sharp pain radiated from his bad shoulder. The strap tightened around his wrist.

"Physical indicators of distress detected," Sam said. "Do you require assistance?"

The creature's thrashing diminished, but it continued to drag Randall along. His feet plowed through loose sediment until they finally struck solid rock. The muscles of his thighs and calves screamed with exertion. Something coiled around his leg again. He glanced down to see Ikaros there, paws braced against the rock as though helping Randall hold firm.

A powerful hand settled on Randall's shoulder.

Dracchus entered Randall's peripheral vision and reached forward with his free hand to grasp the harpoon tether. Spreading his tentacles over the rock, he pulled, reclaiming a bit of slack on the line.

The monster renewed its struggles, clouding the water with crimson.

The hand on Randall's shoulder moved up, tapping him at the base of the skull before Dracchus extended his arm and pointed at the impaled creature.

Randall nodded. Removing his wrist from the loop, he handed the harpoon gun to Dracchus and drew his knife from its sheath on his thigh. He forced his breathing to steady. Without pausing long enough to overthink it, he pulled himself along the tether, avoiding the creature's waving tail. Before he reached the small, toothy mouth, he released the line and swam over its head.

Dropping onto its back, he wrapped his legs around the creature's body to anchor himself in place. Its thrashing strengthened. Gritting his teeth, he raised the knife and slammed it down. The blade punched into the creature's hide just behind its skull.

The monster convulsed and abruptly halted its struggles, turning slowly onto its side.

Randall tugged his knife free and returned to Dracchus as the kraken pulled the carcass closer. A wispy trail of red flowed in the monster's wake, reminding Randall of campfire smoke drifting away on the breeze.

Releasing the spool from the underside of the gun, Dracchus handed the weapon to Randall and wound the line around his hand several times. The kraken nodded, pushed himself up from the bottom, and swam toward the Facility. Randall fell into place beside him. Ikaros swam between them, paws paddling frantically as he banked and spun in a display of underwater acrobatics.

Randall cast a glance back at the dead creature. *So much for fish and bottom feeders.*

The Facility's buildings were dark shapes at the edge of Randall's vision, distinguished more by the lights glowing on their exteriors than by their own forms. Randall doubted he and Dracchus had gone more than half a kilometer to reach the seaweed forest. That meant potential prey — and other predators — lurked within eyeshot of the kraken's home. It was an oddly comforting realization. As different as things were down here, some of the fundamentals — the beauty, the bounty, and the ceaseless danger — were much the same as on land.

Randall's stomach lurched as they proceeded straight off the rise. The bottom fell away below them, and for an instant, his body tensed in anticipation of the downward pull of gravity. It didn't come.

Ikaros settled his paws on Randall's back and rode with him to the Facility.

Two figures floated before the entry door, growing more distinct as Randall neared. Melaina and Rhea, both smiling. The child mimicked Randall's wave.

Rhea caught his gaze and flashed maroon over her skin.

Heat flowed outward from Randall's chest, rippling along his limbs. He knew what that color meant.

"Elevated heartrate detected," Sam said. "Would you—"

"No, Sam. Be quiet."

Randall *wanted* what that color meant.

# CHAPTER 7

*P*ride welled within Rhea as the males swam back toward the Facility. Dracchus was the one hauling their kill, but it was Randall who drew her attention.

Melaina surged past Rhea, and Ikaros pushed off Randall's back to meet the youngling. They swirled around one another, two children at play, producing a cloud of bubbles.

Rhea moved away from the pressurization chamber door, stopping in front of Randall. His body was encased in one of the skin-tight diving suits, accenting his pleasing form. Her eyes paused briefly on his growing erection.

She grinned and met his gaze.

He could not speak to her underwater, and he could not sign like a kraken, but the light in his eyes said all Rhea needed to know.

She'd waited weeks for this moment. Randall's worth had been apparent to Rhea from the beginning, but her word would never have been enough. He had to prove himself capable to the other kraken. Had to prove that he could provide, that he could contribute. This would serve as that proof for most of her people.

More importantly, it would serve as proof to Randall.

Regardless of what any of them thought, Rhea wanted him.

Drifting closer to him, she placed a hand upon his chest, slid an arm around his neck, and coiled a fore tentacle around each of his legs. She tilted her head forward and pressed it against his mask, locking her eyes with his.

The tip of his tongue slipped out and trailed over his lips as he placed his hands on her hips. Heat flared within her core. She swayed her hips, rocking them back and forth to brush her closed slit against his hardness.

His grip on her tightened.

Were he kraken, he'd know what her movements meant. He'd already be sliding into her, connecting their bodies as he joined in the mating dance. But he was human, unable to survive in the water without his suit, and he knew little of their ways.

Rhea would show him what she could.

She moved her tentacles up his back and over his body as she continued to gyrate her hips. Randall's lips parted, and his chest rose and fell rapidly, swelling against her breasts. His blue eyes darkened in desire.

His brows fell suddenly, and he gritted his teeth. His mouth moved as though he were speaking, but Rhea couldn't hear anything. Shaking his head, he gently broke the contact between their bodies, took her hand, and pointed toward the door.

Rhea tilted her head and flashed maroon.

Randall nodded and gestured to the door again, tugging her toward it.

She grinned as excitement crackled through her. Turning

away, she sought Melaina, finding the youngling and the prixxir beside Dracchus. Rhea signaled the large kraken.

*Watch them?*

Dracchus nodded and glanced at Melaina, motioning for her to follow. Accompanied by Ikaros, they hauled the kill toward one of the alternate entrances.

The light above the Facility's main entrance flashed green and the door opened. Randall led Rhea inside, drawing her closer and wrapping an arm around her waist as the door closed and the water began to drain from the chamber. Once his head was above water, he tore off the mask and pulled the hood down.

"Finally." Randall claimed her mouth in a scalding kiss.

Rhea wrapped her arms around him, returning the kiss with equal hunger, craving his taste.

His mouth left hers to trail along her chin and jaw, moving toward her siphon. The stubble on his cheeks scraped her skin, but it only heightened her arousal. Her breath quickened.

"Randall," she rasped.

Keeping one arm around her waist, he moved his other hand to the side of her neck and placed his thumb along her jaw, tilting her head back to access the place between her neck and shoulder. Shivers ran over her flesh, and her breasts and sex ached with need.

When he bit, she gasped, eyes flaring wide, and nearly crested from the shock of pleasure-pain. His tongue followed, soothing the spot. She grazed her claws over his back and pulled him closer.

"Pressurization complete," the computer said, but the words were muted through Rhea's haze of lust.

Randall slapped the button beside the interior door and didn't break contact with Rhea as they moved through. They stumbled;

Randall's back hit the wall, and she fell against his chest, but he recovered quickly and guided her into another kiss.

"A room," Randall said against her mouth.

Rhea growled in frustration, inwardly cursing humans and their need for privacy. But it was warranted now — if another female were to come upon them and so much as glance at Randall, Rhea would be tempted to gouge out that female's eyes.

She pulled away from him and hurried down the hallway, passing countless doors and wishing his den were closer.

Randall abruptly grabbed her hand and tugged her into a darkened room. Pushing her against the wall, he pressed his body to hers. Rhea released a startled breath.

"I can't wait any longer," he rasped.

Before she could reply, his mouth fell over hers again, and his hands slid up her sides to cover her breasts. Rhea arched into his touch with a moan. She grasped his arms, and her tentacles writhed over the floor as he caressed and pinched her nipples. Her slit parted, and she pressed her pelvis against his hardened cock, desperate to feel him inside her.

As he kissed her, she tugged at his suit, growling against his lips when the material wouldn't tear beneath her claws.

"Remove this, human! *Now!*"

He laughed and lifted a hand. The circular device on his chest glowed for a moment when his fingers brushed over it, and the suit loosened. Rhea wasted no time in shoving the material down, baring his arms and torso, using her tentacles to peel it past his waist and off his legs. She would relish his body another time. She'd already waited too long. Right now, she *needed* him.

She wrapped her hand around his shaft the moment it sprang free. The humor faded from Randall's expression, and he hissed through clenched teeth as he slammed a hand onto the wall behind her to brace himself. She brushed the pad of her thumb over the head of the hot, smooth column of flesh, spreading the moisture seeping from its tip.

Rhea looked up and met his eyes, which were shrouded in shadow save for two pinpoints of reflected light from the hallway. Her slit opened fully. She guided the head of his cock to her sex and released him.

He cupped the back of her head with his hand and held her gaze. His eyes burned with possession. "Now you are *mine*," he said and thrust into her.

Rhea shuddered. Her sex clenched around his shaft, pulling him deeper. He stretched her, filled her, completed her.

"Ah, fuck!" Randall growled beside her ear.

She smoothed her hands over his shoulders and held him close. Her fore tentacles slid up his legs, suction cups tasting his skin as they moved to curve over his backside, the tip of one brushing the base of his spine. He trembled, and his subtle vibrations transferred into her. She turned her head and nipped his ear.

"Mate with me," she whispered huskily.

He drew his hips back, and the glide of his cock was exquisite, topped only when he thrust into her again. He repeated the motion again, and again, increasing his speed with each shove. His mouth captured hers in a devouring kiss as their bodies became physical chaos, a tangle of limbs, a mingling of desperate breaths. Rhea could scarce tell where she ended and Randall began.

He pinched and stroked her nipple with one hand, keeping the other against the wall. He ravaged her mouth, her body, marking her as his inside and out.

The ripples of sensation moving through her intensified to a wave of pleasure that flooded her core with heat. Her entire body tensed, and her sex fluttered, gripping him tighter.

Randall's head fell back, and the cords of his neck strained. His muscles locked as his thrusts faltered. The heat inside her suddenly roared into an inferno. He growled, the sound continuing even after his lips found hers again. Rhea lost sense of her surroundings, of herself, of *everything*; only the two of them remained, sharing this moment.

Their connection continued as the aftershocks of her climax pulsed through her. She wasn't willing to release him yet. Tentacles coiled around his waist and legs, she held him close, smiling as she nuzzled his cheek.

"I ought to kick myself for waiting," he said.

Rhea chuckled, smile widening into a grin. "Some things are worth waiting for. Macy told me that. Besides, you can make it up to me."

"Yes, they are, and yes, I will." He turned his head toward the door, and the diffused light from the hallway cast his face in a soft glow. "I don't know if I'm doing this right, but... Rhea, will you share my den?"

Rhea cupped his face with her hands. "Yes. I will share your den if you would have me for a mate."

"Your one and only," he replied, settling his palms on the small of Rhea's back to draw her closer. His cock slid deeper into her. "You're mine, remember?"

"Yes," she hissed, dropping her hands to his shoulders.

"Think we should head to our room before I start making it up to you?"

"No." She twisted, shoving him back against the wall without disconnecting their bodies. "You will do so here and now, human."

Randall laughed. "Gladly."

74

Movement at Randall's feet stirred him from sleep. He fought through the weight of his grogginess to lift his head off the pillow to look at Rhea. She lay alongside him, head on his shoulder, limbs intertwined with his. The room was dark save for the dim glow of the light over the bathroom door, but his eyes had adjusted well enough to make out the basics of her features.

He turned his attention toward the foot of the bed.

Ikaros stood there with spine fin raised and whiskers back, staring toward the door. He released a long, low growl. Randall squeezed his eyes shut and ran a hand over them to force away some of their blurriness.

When he opened them again, he swung his gaze to the doorway. A large, dark shape blocked it from view.

A *moving* shape.

Randall jolted up into a sitting position, disentangling his legs from Rhea's tentacles and swinging them over the side of the bed.

At the corner of his vision, Ikaros leapt off the bed, hurtling toward the dark figure.

Rhea woke with a startled sound as Randall grabbed his pistol from the nightstand. The dark figure snarled and spat a curse; the deep voice could only belong to a male kraken. Gripping his weapon in both hands, Randall spun toward the male.

"Lights on," he said. The overhead light blazed to life. He squinted against the glare for the second it took his eyes to adjust.

Ikaros yelped as the kraken tore him off and hurled him across the room. Randall recognized the kraken — Volk, the one who'd come on to Rhea that day in the mess hall.

"Ikaros!" Melaina cried from her corner.

"Stay where you are, Melaina!" Rhea yelled. She was already off the bed, standing between the male kraken and her daughter.

Volk bared his teeth. Fresh scratches and small bite wounds oozed blood on his chest and face, almost indiscernible from his crimson skin, and his furious eyes were focused on Randall.

There were a hundred reasons for and against shooting. Randall didn't have time to consider any of them before the kraken lunged.

Randall fired a single shot. The boom dominated the room, as deafening as thunder in the small space, and then the pistol was knocked out of his hold by Volk's backhand swing. The male kraken's other arm followed, hitting Randall in the chest.

It felt like he'd been charged by a full-grown krull. The breath burst from his lungs as he was flung backward. His legs hit the side of the bed, and he fell atop it on his back.

The lights inside the room flashed, accompanied by a blaring alarm.

"Firearms discharged in Cabins Hall C, room six," the

Computer announced. "All active security personnel be advised, firearms discharged."

Gulping for air, Randall twisted, looking for the pistol, but Volk was on him too quickly. The kraken slashed downward with his claws, and Randall shifted his torso, narrowly avoiding the blow. Volk's eyes were like twin infernos. Blood trickled from a bullet hole on his abdomen.

Volk put his hands around Randall's throat and leaned his immense weight forward. The bed groaned, as though making up for Randall's current inability to make a sound. His throat would be crushed under the strength of those hands. As his vision blurred, Randall desperately jabbed a fist at the wound on Volk's abdomen.

The kraken grunted and pushed Randall further down. The bedding covered Randall's ears, muffling the sound of the alarms. After two more blows, Randall pressed his fingers into the hole, raking at the slick, torn flesh inside with his nails.

Roaring in pain, Volk lifted Randall off the bed and hurled him aside.

Randall bounced off the other side and hit the floor hard, face-first.

"Randall!" Melaina called.

Head spinning, he pushed himself up off the floor and looked to the child. She remained huddled in the corner on her little pallet, eyes wide and fearful, with Ikaros clutched in her arms. He braced an arm on the mattress and drew himself onto his knees.

The bed creaked as Volk moved over it, approaching Randall. "No human will have our fem—"

His words were choked off as Rhea released a shriek so full of fury that Randall's blood ran cold and launched herself at Volk.

Her momentum slammed the male kraken into the wall. In an

instant, they became a writhing mass of tentacles and slashing claws, spraying blood onto the bedding beneath them.

There was no doubt that Volk was larger and stronger than Rhea, but her ferocity seemed to have tipped the balance in her favor — at least for now.

Sucking in a ragged breath that made his ribs hurt more, Randall turned his attention to the floor, scanning for the pistol. If he jumped into the fray, he'd be torn to shreds. He could only help her if he was armed. His heart pounded in his chest, each beat almost as loud as the gunshot had been and yet barely audible over the alarms.

How long before Volk overpowered her?

Movement from his peripheral vision caused Randall to jerk to the side, ready to mount whatever defense he was able.

Melaina stared up at him with large eyes. She lifted her hands, the pistol resting on her flattened palms.

Randall's sigh of relief was almost as painful as his deep inhalation a moment before. He accepted the pistol from her and, somehow, managed a smile. "Go back to Ikaros, okay?"

She nodded and scurried off.

Randall turned back to the fight, and his heart skipped a beat.

The battling kraken had tumbled off the bed. Volk was poised over Rhea, hands wrapped around her neck and tentacles restraining her limbs. Her thrashing seemed unable to break his hold. Crimson trickled from numerous cuts and scratches on her skin; Volk sported at least twice as many wounds, including a bullet hole on his lower back — an exit wound.

He was going to kill her.

"You betray us all by choosing our enemies over your own kind!" Volk said.

Rhea snarled and renewed her struggles.

Randall rounded the bed and pressed the barrel of the pistol to the base of Volk's skull. The kraken stiffened.

"Get the fuck off her," Randall commanded. "*Now.*"

The male kraken didn't move, but Randall felt the intention, felt the unseen coiling of Volk's muscles.

"I know what you're thinking," Randall said. "You're fast. But I guarantee you're not faster than my trigger finger. Not in this situation."

"You are not worthy of her. You are weak. You are filth."

"And you're dumber than a krull in heat, but I didn't hold that against you. What she deems worthy isn't your business, whether you can see past your prejudices or not."

Volk growled just as the door opened. Jax and Arkon rushed inside, hesitating for only an instant before they moved into action. Within a few seconds, they'd separated Volk from Rhea, and Jax forced Volk onto the floor face-down, restraining him with arms and tentacles.

"Find Dracchus," Jax said to Arkon.

Arkon nodded and turned backed toward the exit, coming to an abrupt halt. Macy and Aymee stood just outside the doorway.

"We told you to remain within the room!" Arkon said.

"Are they okay?" Macy asked, peering past the kraken. "Rhea? Melaina?"

Rhea rose, eyes narrowed on Volk, lips pulled back in distaste. "I am well," she replied without looking away from the male.

"Stay back," Arkon said to Macy and Aymee. He pressed a button beside the door, activating a holoscreen, and flitted through several options. After a few moments, the alarms turned off and the lights reverted to normal.

"Security alert in Cabins Hall C, room six has been cleared," the computer declared cheerfully. "Please resume your normal duties."

With a final frown for Aymee and Macy, Arkon left.

"Go back to Sarina, Macy," Jax said, "and lock the door."

Macy hesitated, gaze shifting to Rhea and Randall before settling on Jax. "Be careful."

Jax nodded to her, and for an instant, Randall saw worry flicker over the kraken's features.

She disappeared into the hallway.

Randall closed the remaining distance between himself and Rhea, pistol dangling in one hand; Jax's prowess wasn't enough to convince Randall to put his weapon down. His chest throbbed, his throat burned, and the shallowest of breaths caused a sharp ache, but his only concern was for Rhea. Her skin had returned to its normal gray, making her numerous cuts and the crimson splattered over her stand out even more.

"Are you really okay?" he asked.

She shook her hands, flicking blood from her claws. "I will heal."

Randall curled a finger beneath her chin and turned her face toward him. "You're sure?"

Her eyes finally met his, and some of their heat dissipated. "I will heal, Randall," she said again, but softer this time. She reached for him, but pulled back with a frown when she saw the blood on her hands.

"What about you, Randall?" Aymee asked from the doorway, features drawn in concern.

"I can still breathe," he replied, "so it can't be that bad, right?"

Something bumped his free hand. He glanced down to the bed him to see Ikaros. The prixxir nudged Randall's palm with his snout, chirruping softly.

Randall crouched, lifted the prixxir into his arms, and stood up again. Ikaros made small, contented sounds. If it weren't for Ikaros, Randall might never have woken up.

"Can I come in to check on them?" Aymee asked.

"Keep a wide distance," Jax replied.

Volk began to speak, but Jax tightened his arm around the other kraken's throat, cutting off the words.

Aymee stepped into the room, keeping as far from Jax and Volk as possible as she made her way toward Randall. She raised her hands to his chest.

Rhea growled, inserting herself between Randall and Aymee.

"Easy," Randall soothed, settling a hand on Rhea's shoulder and gently drawing her back. "It's okay. She's a healer, remember?"

Scowling, Rhea looked away.

"It's okay, Rhea," Aymee said with a smile. "Arkon gets this way, too. I'm just going to check him and make sure he's not seriously injured."

Randall lifted his palm from Rhea's shoulder and took her hand in his, guiding her to stand at his side. "You already claimed me, Rhea. I'm yours. No need to worry."

Lips pressed tightly together, Rhea nodded curtly, motioning for Melaina to join her. The child came immediately and tucked herself against her mother.

"Are you okay, Randall?" Melaina asked softly.

"I'll be fine, kid." He grunted and winced as Aymee's prodded his ribs with her fingers.

"Some serious bruising, and it's going to hurt for a while, but I don't think anything is broken. We'll have to look with the scanner to be sure," Aymee said.

Voices from the hallway called everyone's attention to the door. Arkon and Dracchus entered one after the other, both dripping wet. Several more kraken filled the doorway a moment later, but Arkon blocked their entry.

Dracchus moved to Rhea without so much as a glance at Volk. "How badly are you wounded?"

Rhea lifted her chin, meeting Dracchus's gaze. "I will heal."

The large kraken studied her carefully, assessing the damage. Randall did the same. There was a faint trembling in her hands now, suggesting that her pain was greater than she'd let on, and her skin seemed a shade paler than usual.

Dracchus's fury was plain; it radiated from him like waves of roiling heat and shaped his expression into something murderous. He glanced at Randall, an unspoken question in his eyes.

"I'll heal, too. Just slower," Randall said.

Rhea and Dracchus met one another's gazes, and the large male nodded.

"Volk has invaded this den," Rhea said, voice raised, "endangering myself and my youngling, and attacked my mate."

Based on the hushed voices in the hallway, there were more kraken gathered than Randall had realized. A tense silence followed the torrent of whispers.

Volk strained against Jax's hold, but Jax only tightened his grip.

Dracchus turned toward the doorway, through which numerous kraken peered into the room. "Volk has betrayed our people by disregarding the things we hold most important," he said. He moved to the pinned kraken, and he and Jax dragged Volk off the floor. "Rhea has made her accusation. The proof of it is plain. Volk has—"

"Enough!" someone shouted from the corridor. There was a brief commotion as Kronus shoved his way through the crowd and came face-to-face with Arkon. Dracchus and Jax dragged Volk in front of the doorway, blocking it from Randall's view.

Rhea growled, muscles tensing. Randall gave her hand a squeeze. He hoped the gesture was enough to communicate with her — *I'm here; we're okay; we made it through this one.*

"What is the meaning of this?" Kronus demanded. "Allow me to pass!"

"Do you have something to say on Volk's behalf?" Dracchus asked. Though his tone remained even, his black skin lightened just enough to tinge red.

Kronus flicked a glance at Volk. "He was seeking to entice Rhea. She should mate one of our own kind, not a human. It is obvious that the human attacked, just as he attacked us in the Mess."

Dracchus's next move was made with such deliberate slowness that it was terrifying — despite his immense anger, his control was unbroken. He shifted his arm back, extending a clawed finger to point toward Rhea, and twisted his torso to allow Kronus a clear view of the female.

Kronus's eyes widened, and several emotions swept over his features in rapid succession. Startlement, anger, fear. "You attacked one of our females?"

"Do you have anything else to say on his behalf?" Dracchus's voice was low.

"He acted of his own accord," Kronus grated, skin reddening, "and with great foolishness. But do you see what these humans have done? They have disgraced and tainted our home and will be the destruction of our kind if we allow this to continue. They are turning kraken against kraken, now."

Despite the stomach-churning hatred dripping from Kronus's words, Randall couldn't help feeling guilty for his part in all of this. He'd intended to hunt kraken when he'd traveled to Macy and Aymee's hometown. Had Cyrus won the confrontation in the submarine pen, the rangers would've continued searching for kraken, wouldn't have stopped until these people were wiped out.

But that outcome had been avoided, at least for now. Were what-ifs acceptable justification for murder? Did Randall's culpability in what might have been mean he didn't deserve to live?

*No.*

"The only destruction I see," said another kraken behind Kronus — Ector, one of the older kraken males, "is what you and your followers have wrought. These humans have done nothing except give our people hope." He nodded toward Jax. "Hope that we may yet prosper."

"They foul our bloodline!" Kronus said. "They have ever been our enemies and would destroy our kind if given the opportunity!"

"Are you forgetting that all of you are part human?" Aymee asked. "It's in your DNA."

"And each of the humans here has saved the life of a kraken," Arkon added, looking to Aymee.

"You have had your say, Kronus," Dracchus said. "Now Volk may have his."

Jax finally eased his hold on Volk's neck. The restrained kraken sagged slightly and sucked in a ragged breath.

"We will not remain idle while humans mate with our people," Volk rasped. "We will not allow our enemies to dwell among us, and we will not allow our ways to falter." He looked over his shoulder to glare at Randall; the blood flowing from his wounds had slowed significantly, but that only made them more pronounced.

Ikaros shifted in Randall's hold and growled at Volk.

"Will anyone deny Volk's treachery?" Dracchus asked.

Silence fell over the crowd.

Kronus's features were strained, and he averted his eyes from Volk. It seemed even he couldn't deny that — whatever the motivations — his follower had done wrong.

"Kronus!" Volk called, fighting Jax's hold. "I didn't attack her!"

"So, she scratched herself?" Aymee asked.

Volk's skin went red, and he struggled harder. Jax tightened his arm around Volk's neck. Within a few seconds, the struggles ceased.

"Ector, what would the punishment have been in your day?" Dracchus asked.

"For violence against a female, especially endangering a youngling? Death."

Volk paled, and his short, labored breaths quickened.

"Our world is changing, and we must change with it," Dracchus said. "Volk shall be exiled from our home, never to return. Should he show his face here again, it will be within the right of any kraken to end his life. Does anyone oppose my judgment?"

Once more, silence fell over the gathered kraken, allowing the sound of Randall's heartbeat to fill his ears. He counted eleven thumps before Dracchus spoke again.

"It is thus settled." Dracchus took Volk from Jax and forced him out of the room. The other kraken, Kronus included, moved out of his way and dispersed once he'd passed.

When only Aymee, Arkon, and Jax remained, Rhea slumped, releasing a shaky breath.

Randall hurriedly wrapped an arm around her waist and caught her weight; though he was able to keep her upright, she was far heavier than a human, and he wouldn't be able to move her far on his own.

"Let's get her to the infirmary," Aymee said.

"Mother?" Melaina asked with wide eyes.

"She just needs some rest, kid." Randall looked to Jax and Arkon. "Would you guys mind giving me a hand?"

Rhea cupped Randall's cheek and turned his face toward her. "You are worth the fight, my hunter."

Randall pressed his forehead to hers. She would have fought to the death to protect him, and he for her, and that knowledge hit him hard. "So are you."

# CHAPTER 9

*M*elaina's laughter mixed with Rhea's as they squirmed upon the bed, each struggling to catch her breath as Randall kept them pinned, assaulting them with his clawless fingers. Tickling was an intense feeling; forceful, overwhelming, almost painful, while at the same time eliciting a strange thrill. She could have broken his hold if she chose to, but hearing her daughter's laughter — and her own — she'd allowed the torture to continue.

Ikaros chirruped, nimbly bounding between arms and tentacles.

"Stop! Stop!" Melaina cried, rolling from beneath Randall and dropping onto the floor, gasping and giggling. "Ikaros, to me! Protect me!"

The prixxir hopped off the bed and onto Melaina, turning so his waving tail brushed over her cheeks.

Randall stilled his hands. He grinned down at Rhea from his position above her, his thighs straddling her sides. His eyes dipped, and Rhea knew by the heat in them that his thoughts had taken a turn from playful to passionate.

Chest heaving, Rhea smiled. She ran the backs of her fingers down his bare arms and raised a pair of tentacles to caress his shoulders and back.

Randall cleared his throat and glanced over the side of the bed. "So, the traitorous prixxir is siding with you?"

"He will protect me!" Melaina replied. "He knows who feeds him extras."

"Keep feeding him those extras and he'll be too fat to protect anything."

Rhea turned her face toward Melaina. "You best go to Macy for protection before Randall catches you again."

Melaina's eyes rounded as they shot up to Randall. "No! No more tickles!"

Randall extended an arm toward the youngling, waggling his fingers with exaggerated menace.

She shrieked, leaping up from the floor and quickly moving to the door. She pounded on the button and was out before it had fully opened. Ikaros remained where he was, head cocked, glancing from the open door to Randall.

"You, too! Go on," Randall said.

Ikaros chirruped.

"I'm fine. Go look out for Melaina." Reaching down, Randall patted the prixxir's head and nudged the creature along. Ikaros brushed his cheek against Randall's palm before scurrying off after Melaina, claws clicking on the floor. The door closed several seconds later.

A slow grin spread across Rhea's lips as she ran an open hand down Randall's chest.

He covered her hand with his own. "You know it excites me when you let me win."

"The hunter has conquered his prey," she said, her other hand slipping between their bodies to grasp his hard shaft through his clothing.

He laughed, though the sound ended in a lustful groan. "More like the hunter has *become* the prey." He lowered his hands to her hips and slid them upward.

"Mmm." Rhea closed her eyes and stroked his cock as his palms covered her breasts. She'd been surprised when she first learned that human males always extruded, hardening when aroused, but she found enjoyment in having access to Randall without having to coax his shaft free.

"You make it pretty difficult to keep my hands to myself," Randall rasped.

"So keep them on me, human." She opened her eyes to meet his gaze.

"Don't have to tell me twice." He leaned down, and his lips joined his hands in caressing her flesh, trailing heat across her chest and up her neck.

She arched into his touch. Desire flooded her, and she opened beneath him, slit parting. Releasing his shaft, she slipped her hands into his pants to grasp his backside.

"Now, Randall," she commanded as he nipped her nipple with his flat teeth.

He shifted a hand to the waistband of his pants and shoved them down. Gripping his erection, he guided it to her sex. He groaned as he slid inside her, taking his time, but it was not what Rhea wanted. She needed to feel him; *all* of him. She needed him to lose control, to let him bring them both to rapture.

Squeezing his ass, she pulled him toward her, forcing him to thrust swift and deep. She moaned, clenching around him.

Randall braced his arms on either side of her head and cursed. "I won't last long if you keep that up."

Rhea chuckled, stroking her tentacles along his back and legs. "Slow later. Conquer your prey now."

"Challenge accepted." Randall grinned before pulling his hips back and slamming into her, sending a burst of pleasure through every part of her being.

～

*R*hea rested upon Randall's chest as he slept, her head tucked beneath his chin. His legs were spread to accommodate the rest of her, and her tentacles continued to lazily stroke over them, suction cups tasting the salt and sweat on his skin. She smiled, flattening her palm over his chest. His heart beat steadily within.

A single heart. A caring, wonderful, human heart, so strong and full that it easily equaled the three beating within her.

She couldn't remember ever feeling so content. She had friends. She had a *family*. It was a new concept to the kraken, one she and many others were embracing.

Randall tightened his arms around her and released a long, loud exhalation.

Her hunter had awakened.

She tilted her head back and kissed his neck.

He hummed appreciatively, the sound vibrating through his chest and making her skin tingle. "Been awake long?" he asked, voice thick with sleep.

"No," she replied. "You didn't sleep long enough, human."

"Maybe I wanted a fourth round."

Rhea grinned, and she could already feel him hardening beneath her.

Randall inhaled deeply, chest swelling, and let the breath out slowly. "I want to join with you, Rhea."

Chuckling, she propped herself up with arms braced on either side of him. "I would like slow, now," she said, leaning forward to brush her lips across his. "Sensual."

He laughed and shook his head, placing a hand on her cheek. "So would I, but that's not what I meant."

Her brow lowered in confusion. "I do not understand. You said you wish to join with me."

"Yeah, but…" His tongue slipped out and ran over his lips. "So, you claimed me as your mate the way your people do, and we're sharing a den. When my people talk about *joining*, it's sort of like those things. It's choosing a mate for the rest of your life. And I want that, with you. I want you and Melaina to be the biggest parts of the rest of my life."

Rhea's hearts stilled, and when they beat again, there was a tightness in her chest. She pressed a hand between her breasts as though that could take away the ache. Randall covered her hand with his own.

"Join with me, Rhea. Be mine," he said.

She released a shaky breath and smiled. "Hunter, you were mine from the moment you arrived here." She lowered her face to his. "And I was ever yours."

Randall grinned and cupped the back of her head, bringing her mouth down. He kissed her deeply, holding her close, and when he withdrew his lips he met her gaze.

"Shall we join that fourth time, now?" she asked.

He laughed and flipped her onto her back. He held her gaze as he trailed his mouth down her body, hands skimming over her sides.

"What are you doing?" she asked as his lips neared her slit.

"Ensuring my mate is the best-loved female in the sea."

Rhea gasped, and all thought fled her mind except the pleasure of Randall's tongue. Her cries ensured everyone in the Facility knew just how well loved she was.

# AUTHOR'S NOTE

We just wanted to shout out a huge thank you to everyone who helped support us and the fellow authors of the Pets in Space 3 Anthology, Embrace the Passion. We were able to donate $2,700 to Hero Dogs, a service which helps disabled veterans and first responders with trained dogs. It was such an amazing experience to be part of this project.

Below is a picture of our beloved Ikaros, sketched by Nyssa Juneau. Isn't he adorable?

Thank you all again, and we hope you continue to enjoy our Kraken Series!

# ABOUT THE AUTHOR

Tiffany Roberts is the pseudonym for Tiffany and Robert Freund, a husband and wife writing duo. Tiffany was born and bred in Idaho, and Robert was a native of New York City before moving across the country to be with her. The two have always shared a passion for reading and writing, and it was their dream to combine their mighty powers to create the sorts of books they want to read. They write character driven sci-fi and fantasy romance, creating happily-ever-afters one monster or alien at a time.

Website:
**https://authortiffanyroberts.wordpress.com**
Facebook:
**https://www.facebook.com/AuthorTiffanyRoberts**
BookBub:
**https://www.bookbub.com/authors/tiffany-roberts**

**Sign up for our Newsletter!**

36661247R00063

Made in the USA
Lexington, KY
16 April 2019